The Tree from the Land Beyond

Shelagh Jones

WOLFHOUND PRESS
Celebrating 25 Years

First published in 1999 by
Wolfhound Press Ltd
68 Mountjoy Square
Dublin 1, Ireland
Tel: (353-1) 874 0354
Fax: (353-1) 872 0207

The Arts Council
An Chomhairle Ealaíon

Wolfhound Press receives financial assistance from The Arts
Council/An Chomhairle Ealaíon, Dublin, Ireland.

British Library Cataloguing in Publication Data
A catalogue record for this book is available from the British Library.

ISBN 0-86327-668-7

10 9 8 7 6 5 4 3 2 1

J84, 603 £4.99

Cover Illustration: Aileen Caffrey
Cover Design: Sally Mills-Westley
Typesetting: Wolfhound Press
Printed in the UK by Cox & Wyman Ltd, Reading, Berks.

The Tree from the Land Beyond

Shelagh Jones was born of Irish-Scottish parentage in London, shortly before Hitler blitzed it. Much of her early life was spent on the move. Eventually she returned to Ireland, to Co. Wicklow, where she lived for many years. A trained teacher of drama, she was involved in the amateur drama movement in Scotland, England and Ireland and, until recently, directed plays. Her interest in nature goes back to childhood, as does her interest in myth and legend. She is the author of three books for children: *Save the Unicorns* and *The DerrynaLushca Dragon* (The Children's Press) and *The Silver Chalice* (Wolfhound Press). Shelagh Jones is a mother and grandmother. She lives in Co. Limerick.

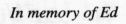

In memory of Ed

Contents

"Everything's Wrong!"

'*H*e could have got a good job at the Factory,' said Aunt Mary. She'd said it before.

'He wouldn't darken their doors,' said Mother — not for the first time.

'Sean has done very nicely out of it,' said Aunt Mary, 'and no harm done.' She sipped her tea.

'Sean must do what Sean must do,' Mother replied firmly. 'My Liam is different.'

'You can say that again,' sniffed Aunt Mary. 'Sean says it was always so — when they were boys, even. Is there another drop in the pot?'

'Help yourself,' snapped Mother.

A pause — truce! — while Aunt Mary poured the tea ....

'But *America*!' she said, settling herself more comfortably to pick up the threads of the argument. 'For two whole years!'

'There's many a one gone before,' countered Mother, 'and made their fortunes.'

The argument rumbled on, in undertones, part of the background noise, like the guttering of the flames in the grate and the ticking of the old clock on the mantel. Bridget sucked the end of her Biro and studied her sum. She was having to blink hard to prevent the numbers swimming in front of her eyes. Automatically, her hand sought the soft fur of Timkit, curled on her knees. The cat's purrs mingled with the other sounds of the room.

'Seven fives are thirty-five,' Bridget chanted defensively, 'put down five and carry three ....'

The dispute continued. 'But to leave you and the children ....' Aunt Mary's voice was sanctimonious. 'And the old man!'

'He hasn't left us for good, Mary.' Mother's tone was crisp. 'And can you see Father flying to the States?'

'Well, you know what I think about *that* matter.'

'Yes, I do,' Mother said dryly. 'And you'll not repeat it.' Her words beamed in Bridget's direction like a warning beacon.

Another pause — not so much for a truce as to bring fresh ammunition up to the battle-lines. Bridget crossed out an error and continued to work on her sum.

'Not the only mistake,' she thought bitterly. '*Everything's* wrong!'

Timkit's purrs faded into slumber. The clock took a laboured breath, wheezed and struck nine, its last strike tinny, short, as if the clockwork couldn't quite find the energy to make the full sound.

The chimes drew Mother's mind away from the conflict, back to the calm everyday matters she was fighting to defend. 'Off to bed now, Bridget,' she said. 'Kiss your grandfather.'

'But I haven't finished my homework,' Bridget objected.

'Then you must finish it in the morning.' Mother was firm. For children, sleep was precious, she considered, as was play; to her way of thinking, homework could always wait.

'Where's Michael?' she enquired.

'Out the back, feeding his rabbits.'

'Tell him to come in when you put the cat out,' Mother said easily. 'Say good night to Aunt Mary. Kiss your grandfather,' she repeated.

Bridget closed her books and lifted Timkit, tucking him under her arm, where he hung loose and comfortable like an old fur stole. She had no intention of putting him out, and Mother knew it. An hour later, Timkit would be rescued from under the bedclothes and put out then. It was all part of the family routine.

Mumbling a dutiful 'Good night' to Aunt Mary — who merely nodded — she crossed to the silent figure by the fire.

Grandfather's cheek was bristly, prickly and uncomfortable to touch; the stroke had left his mouth lopsided. Bridget avoided the twisted features. She bent and placed a gentle kiss upon the old man's forehead, where the skin was as soft and wrinkled as it had always been. It felt reassuringly warm, like the well-worn lining of a coat made cosy by the fire before you put it on against the winter. His blue eyes, bright in their pink sockets, left the flames and travelled to meet hers. They had a twinkle deep down which, Bridget guessed, replaced the smile his lips could no longer give.

'Good night, Grandfather,' she whispered. 'Happy dreams!'

Could he hear her? If so, he made no sign. For that matter, was he able to hear the argument going on across the kitchen table? What thoughts were passing behind the soft skin and firm bone of the old man's forehead, she wondered? He didn't speak. Grandfather had said nothing since that dreadful day when it seemed a thunderbolt had been dropped, like a spanner from a careless hand above ....

'He tried to say a few words in the hospital,' Mother had told them, 'but when he realised he was just making ugly noises he gave it up. Ah, sure, what harm?' When it came to her family, Mother could see a benefit in anything. 'He has his memories to sift through. He's had a long life. And a good one.'

'Hardly *good*!' Aunt Mary would have snorted. But, unlike Mother, Aunt Mary was unable to see much good in anyone. How could she guess what might be going on behind the old man's wrinkled brow?

'Straight to bed, now,' Mother said, as Bridget kissed her good night.

The stair was dark, steep and narrow, tucked behind its doorway by the fireplace like a secret in a cupboard. Bridget had no need of light; she knew every board beneath her feet. She trod them carefully, avoiding the creaks.

The cottage was very old. When the wind blew, it didn't resist, but swayed with it. Raindrops had no need to bounce off its roof; they just sank into the deep moss, to help it grow. 'It's not like Aunt Mary's modern bungalow, with its polished floors and its "great amenities",' Bridget thought as she entered her little attic bedroom, with its sloping roof, and reached to switch on the bedside lamp. 'It's much more comfortable, and much more fun. It's home!'

Timkit leapt from her arms to paddle the quilt into the shape he liked before curling up in the light-pool on the bed. Dragging a chair into place, Bridget climbed up to open the skylight so she could listen to the tree.

Listening to Grandfather's tree was an essential part of what Bridget meant by 'home'. Its voice was the first thing she heard each morning; its whispers crept into her dreams at night. To its rhythms, she made up poems and stories.

It was a strange tree. There wasn't another like it in

the district — nor in the whole of Ireland, Bridget had been told. Grandfather had planted it as a sapling many years ago, long before the children — or their parents — had been born. From its roots to the topmost twig, it was the colour of pure silver. It grew straight and tall, rising out of the stones of the yard as if it spurned the ordinary clay. Its silvery leaves glittered in the sunlight; they tinkled like wind-chimes when the breeze blew in a certain way.

'Listen! The tree is singing its song,' Bridget would say to Michael.

'It's only the wind. You do talk rubbish,' he would scoff. But, despite his scorn, Bridget knew that what she said was true. If you listened very carefully you could hear the words, sung in bell-like voices as the wind stirred the branches of the tree:

'Oak is strong, the rowan bright,
Ash is straight and brings the shower,
The yew tree is as old as Time,
But the Silver Tree — she has the Power!'

Leaning far out of the window on windy nights, caught in a silver mesh of movement, Bridget would sing the song too:

'Beech is fair, the birch has grace,
The cherry tree is sweet of flower,
The yew tree is as old as Time,
But the Silver Tree — she has the Power!'

'Where did the tree come from?' Bridget had often asked her grandfather — in those days when he could speak. She had received no proper answer. Leaning on his rake or his pitchfork or his shovel, Grandfather would simply cock his head towards the distant hills. 'The land beyond,' was all he would tell her.

Pulling the skylight further open, Bridget peered down into the yard. A small dark figure was moving about in the twilight below. Presently she heard a soft twang and a thud, and a stone tipped the boundary wall to land on the road.

'He's playing with that silly catapult again,' she thought crossly. 'Not that he hits much!' Michael's aim wasn't very good. Besides, to give him credit, at least he (unlike his friends) didn't shoot at anything that was alive. All the same, his new aggression angered her.

'Michael!' she hissed, with all the authority of an older sister (by one year!) 'Come in at once. It's well past bedtime, Mother says.'

At this, the dark figure melted into the shadow of the wall. Hoisting itself up into the light of the newly risen moon, it turned a pale disc of a face, round as the moon itself, towards her.

'Stop making faces, Michael,' Bridget snapped, guessing correctly what he was doing. She slammed the window, as a stone hit the roof, and leapt down from the chair.

After a while, to her satisfaction, she heard the stairs creaking and Michael entering the room next to hers. She could hear him shuffling about, muttering to himself. Then there was a squeak from the bedsprings on the far side of the wall, followed by silence.

'Are you asleep yet, Michael?' Bridget whispered to a knot in the panelling. More silence. (She was sure she could hear him holding his breath.) Then elaborate snores.

Sighing, Bridget pulled on her pyjamas. She padded over on bare feet to re-open the window. Shifting Timkit's weight, she got into bed. The cat settled back into position and became heavier than before. Beyond the open window the leaves rustled, weaving shifting patterns of moonlight on the bedroom floor. As the wind increased, they took up their song:

'Holly is sharp, and willow soft,
The hawthorn decks a fairy's bower,
Old yew spreads at the churchyard gate,
But the Silver Tree — she has the Power!'

Bridget opened a book and tried to read, but the singing of the tree was catching her attention. Again and again, her eyes were drawn to the urgently skipping patterns on the floor. It was as if they were trying to tell her something. A new verse had been added to the song:

'Oak, ash, and beech, they may unite,
Thorn weave thickets to make men cower,
The forests spread throughout the land —
'Tis the Silver Tree that holds the Power!'

Putting down her book, Bridget leaned back against the pillows and let her mind slip over recent events. Mother was trying so hard to act as if everything was normal .... 'But it's not,' said Bridget. 'It's all wrong. Everything's *wrong*.'

She began to count the disasters, one by one.

First there had been Grandfather's stroke — shockingly sudden, with a terrible effect. It had reduced a bright and active man to something inert and twisted, like a dead stick by the fire.

'He's old,' Mother had told Bridget gently. 'Such things happen.'

'He's not that old,' Bridget had said fiercely. In any case, she noticed that as Mother bustled about, tending to Grandfather's needs, she still spoke to him as she had always done — asking his advice, listening carefully, and nodding as if she heard his answers.

'I wish *I* could hear him,' Bridget fretted. She longed more than anything for the sound of his voice, telling them his stories, singing the old familiar ballads by the fire .... He was no longer able even to whistle to his dog.

His dog! That had been Disaster Number Two. Even now, Bridget could feel a tear creeping down her cheek towards the pillow at the memory. Bewildered, missing his master, old Grip had spent the first few days after the tragedy curled up on the step, as close as he could get to the back door. When Grandfather didn't come out, Grip had taken to wandering. Finally he had wandered towards the Factory, and ....

Bridget clenched her fists, digging her fingernails into her hands. She couldn't bear to think about what had happened. She had cried all night. So had Michael — 'Even though he's changed,' she whispered. 'Even though he won't be friends, won't play the same games any more ....'

The Factory! Hate rose into Bridget's throat, choking her. Sensing it, Timkit uncurled and crept beneath the sheet. 'The Factory! That's what's making everything go wrong,' said Bridget.

Vast and hideous, the Factory stood at the river's edge. It loomed over the village and the surrounding countryside, over their lives, like a threatening beast. Its breath was everywhere — in the hedgerows, in people's gardens, on the washing, on the windows. It even spread a film upon the puddles when it rained. There was no escaping its hundreds of blind eyes, staring sightlessly out of smoky glass; nor its tall chimneys, like overgrown nostrils spewing filth into the air. Around it, all the trees were dying. The grass by its gates was turning yellow in despair.

'It will bring new jobs into the district,' they had been told. It had done nothing of the sort. The workers looking after the 'beast' came from the city, twenty miles away, roaring along the country roads in their cars and leaving just as noisily and hastily at night. Very few locals crossed the causeway to present their passcards at the automatic gates. One of the chosen ones — as Aunt Mary never tired of telling them — was Uncle Sean.

This brought Bridget to the last disaster: their father's sudden and unexpected decision to leave his family and his little farm, to travel to the States. 'To make our fortune,' Mother had told Aunt Mary.

Bridget knew she was only teasing. What did Dad — or any of them — care about fortunes? 'Haven't we plenty as it is?' she said to herself. 'What's more, we were happy.'

Bridget's mind twisted itself into knots as she tried to make sense of it all. There had been half-heard snatches of conversation, coming to an abrupt end when she entered the room. She had caught only a few disjointed words: 'land' ... 'by the river' ... 'the old farm' ... 'deeds' (what did that mean?) ... 'Uncle John' (he had been Grandfather's brother, she recalled). Voices had been raised in anger — her father's, Aunt Mary's (shrill), Uncle Sean's; Mother's calm voice tried to quieten them. Grandfather had once owned land by the river, Bridget knew that .... Finally there had been that big row; the house had shaken with it ....

Whatever the reason for Dad's absence (and Mother wouldn't talk about it), instinct told her it had something to do with the Factory — the Factory and Uncle Sean.

The rustling of the leaves was quieter now. Their song had faded, as if the tree was settling down to sleep.

'At least it never changes,' Bridget thought drowsily. 'It's always the same. It just grows a little every year, and sometimes it has a new nest in its branches. It never even sheds a leaf.'

She closed her eyes.

She slept fitfully. Her dreams were troubled — as well they might be.

Just two miles away, smoke from the Factory curled like a serpent up towards the moon. Outside Bridget's window, a leaf came away from its silver twig. Catching at moonbeams, it fluttered helplessly towards the ground.

The Man in the
Black Limousine

*W*hen Bridget woke the next morning, she had an uneasy feeling that something else was on the point of going wrong. She glanced at her bedside clock. It was only six-thirty; the alarm hadn't gone off yet. Whatever was going to happen, at least she had plenty of time to get her homework finished before breakfast.

Sitting up in bed, she continued where she had left off the night before. The maths was easy — revision, really — so she didn't know why she kept making mistakes. Soon the page began to look very messy. 'Sister Monica will kill me!' thought Bridget. She noticed that she had got Biro marks on the sheets and knew she wouldn't be too popular with Mother, either.

Then she realised why she couldn't concentrate. Beyond the open window, everything was strangely quiet. There was no twittering of birds, no lowing from the cattle in the barn. Outside, the tree stood statue-still — and silent.

Biro poised, book open on her knee, Bridget sat tense. Even on the calmest of days, there was always a rustle or a patter in the leaves. Grandfather used to joke that, if you heard nothing else, you'd surely hear a caterpillar stamp its foot! But this morning, there wasn't a murmur. There was no song. It was as if the tree had been turned to stone in the night.

Flinging back her bedclothes, Bridget was about to take a look when the silence was broken by two sounds.

Neither sound was pleasant. They both had a grating quality that was irritating to the ear. The first was violent and persistent — a sort of angry scraping, flapping noise, as if something trapped in the branches of the tree was fighting to escape. It was accompanied at irregular intervals by a harsh, ill-natured croak.

All senses on the alert, thankful it was daylight, Bridget crept to the window and gradually eased it further open. The air was heavy with unpleasant smells from the Factory. The leaves of Grandfather's tree looked tarnished; they hung limp and lifeless.

Plucking up courage, Bridget leaned out and stared into the branches.

At first she saw nothing at all. Then her eye was caught by something white and moving. It was only a piece of plastic, one of the many which, along with other debris, littered the countryside now that the Factory had come. Feeling angry at the contamination of her precious tree, but somewhat reassured, Bridget was about to withdraw her head when a bough nearby was thrust roughly aside and she found herself facing the biggest, ugliest bird she had ever seen.

It looked something like a rook; but a rook, no matter how rich the pickings, could never achieve such a size. In spite of that, it was obvious that the bird was starving. The way it was attacking the plastic, frantically going over it for any remains of food, told Bridget it was ravenous. It was unhealthy, too: patches of scurfy, bluish skin showed amongst its dusty feathers, and there was an oozing sore under one of its hooded eyes. It had a large, pale beak, warty with carbuncles and twisted out of shape as if the creature had met with a nasty accident. Or perhaps, thought Bridget, it had been hatched deformed .... For a short while she found herself caught up in a baleful yellow stare.

'It's only a bird,' she told herself severely. She began to shout and wave her arms. 'Shoo! Shoo! Shoo!'

It had no effect. If a bird could sneer, this one did. With a venomous look, it opened its crooked bill and hissed at her.

'Michael! Michael!' To Bridget's relief, a rattle at the next window told her that her brother was awake and also watching the intruder. 'Fetch your catapult. Quick!' she screamed — how ashamed she would normally have been of this order!

It was unnecessary. As usual, Michael's catapult was close at hand. With trembling fingers he placed a marble in the sling (no matter where he was, or what he wore — even pyjamas — Michael always had a supply of marbles in his pocket). Steadying himself on the windowsill, he took careful aim and fired.

For once, the shot found its mark. With a gasping croak, the creature took off on clumsy wings and flapped away, leaving the piece of plastic hanging from the branch.

'What was it?' At last, Bridget found her voice.

Michael shrugged. 'Some sort of crow, I suppose,' he replied, his voice full of triumph at his successful shot.

The next moment, both fear and triumph were forgotten. The children leaned out of their open windows and stared at something lying on the ground. Their eyes met across the gable.

Like most red-haired people's (how Bridget envied him! Her hair was a dull mouse-brown), Michael's face was covered with freckles; at that instant, Bridget swore she saw the freckles fade.

Their heads withdrew. On either side of the wall, their feet scrabbled for their slippers. Dressing-gowns were flung on, chairs knocked over, doors left open wide. They pounded down the stairs. At the back door, they collided, but Bridget burst through first to reach the yard.

With a cry of dismay, she dropped to her knees and gathered up the leaves that were scattered on the stones.

'They must have fallen ....' Tilting back her head, she gazed up at the tree — almost as if she could mark the place from which each leaf had come, climb up, and somehow put it back. 'How did it happen?'

'That bird knocked them off, of course.' Michael scuffed a patch of clay with the toe of his slipper. He wasn't feeling as confident as he pretended.

'But it couldn't have. The leaves don't come off. The tree is "ever silver" — that's one of the things that makes it special. Don't you remember? Grandfather said —'

'All trees shed some of their leaves sometimes,' Michael argued, 'even hollies and yews and firs and the like. You see their leaves on the ground.'

'Not *this* tree,' Bridget said stubbornly. 'It's different.'

Michael said nothing. He bent to pick up his marble. It was one of those moments when he missed his dad.

Bridget spread out the leaves and looked at them. There were seven of them. Like those remaining on the tree, they were slightly tarnished and wafer-thin, almost transparent. She stacked them with infinite care and, taking a clean handkerchief from her dressing-gown pocket, stowed them between the folds. She took the handkerchief upstairs; when she got dressed, she tucked it up the sleeve of her school jersey. It was still there when — eventually — she reached school. The leaves remained up her sleeve for the rest of the day — and longer.

As Bridget had anticipated, at school she was in for trouble. It wasn't just a matter of messy homework (Sister Monica was a stickler for neatness in everything); there was also the fact that she had arrived late.

For once it wasn't Michael's fault. She couldn't blame *him*, Bridget thought, fingering the little bundle up her sleeve as she waited in the passageway outside Sister Moira's office ('Martyrs' Walk', the place was called, but there was nothing saintly about those who trod its path). No; Michael had shot ahead, as he so often did nowadays, to 'meet the lads'. Loitering behind, Bridget had watched them dribbling a football along the road. J841603.

But there had been other distractions .... For instance, she had stopped to talk to Bob and the Logman, and she had spent some time with the Logman's jennet.

Bridget loved the Logman's jennet. Jennets, she had been told, were very rare nowadays. This was a perfect specimen — half-donkey, half-pony. It was often to be seen on the road, pulling the Logman's little cart as he went from house to house delivering firewood. The Logman was very proud of it. He kept its skewbald coat spotlessly clean and its harness shining. He oiled its hoofs every day, had it shod regularly, and fed it a pint of Guinness each night before he went to bed. 'Sure, when it rains the creature is kept locked up in its stable,' his neighbours would say. 'It's the Logman himself who pulls the cart.'

While Bob and the Logman chatted, Bridget fumbled in her pocket for a packet of mints and offered one to the jennet. The jennet fastidiously crunched the mint between its yellow teeth. It jangled its silver bit, wrinkled its nose, and jerked its head, but despite this outward show Bridget knew it was enjoying the titbit.

'How's the old man?' the Logman asked. Considering

that he and Grandfather were the same age and had
been boys together, 'old man' was a bit cheeky, but
Bridget let it pass.

'He's as well as may be,' she answered. It was what
she always said; she found that people understood.

The Logman grunted. To a stranger the grunt might
have sounded unsympathetic, but Bridget knew better.
After all, the two men had been schoolmates and life-
long friends; they had played hurley together. It didn't
seem fair, she thought, glancing at the Logman's burly
frame, that he should be so strong and young-looking,
while Grandfather .... Blinking back the tears, she
studied the jennet's sticking-up mane, short and bristly
as a toothbrush, and ran her hand over it.

'Another dead branch,' commented Bob, pulling it
from the hedge. (He was helping out at the farm while
Father was away, as well as keeping the roads tidy in
his usual job of roadman.) 'This ditch is becoming a
little fringe only.'

'It's the same up the road, all the way to Cassidy's.'
The Logman kicked the crumbling twigs with his boot.
'Useless, even for kindling,' he said. 'There's great elms
and oaks just fading away in the woods, leaves twisting up and dropping off like autumn. Dead trees are
good for my business, I'm thinking, but when they're
all gone — what then?'

'Did you hear about Sam Dooley's hens?' Bob asked.

The Logman nodded. 'Only six left,' he said, 'and
the poor man crying like a baby.'

'I heard it was just three.'

Accusingly, both men stared over to where the
Factory, snorting fumes, sank jagged teeth into the
skyline.

Bridget followed their gaze. 'Grandfather's tree is
losing its leaves, too,' she said sadly. But, busy with

their own gloomy thoughts, the men didn't hear her.

'Talking of things happening out of season, did you know that Frosty Meg is in the townland?' Bob asked.

'I did.' The Logman nodded. 'I was talking to her yesterday.'

'What did she say?'

'Nothing much. You can guess why she's here.' The men's voices had sunk low. What they were saying sounded like a conspiracy.

'Why is she here?' The words burst from Bridget's lips before she could prevent them.

The men had forgotten she was there. Alerted, they turned her way.

'Time you were in school,' the Logman told her severely. 'Do those nuns have nothing to teach you?'

'They do, of course.' Sighing, Bridget gave the jennet's neck a final pat and picked up her school-bag.

'Good luck!' the men said as she moved away. Somehow, the familiar wish sounded hollow.

The next person Bridget met was Frosty Meg herself.

Bridget nodded shyly; it would have been rude not to. At the same time she crossed to the other side of the road, making herself as small as possible. The travelling woman, with her odd, wild looks and brightly coloured, loosely flapping clothes, had always frightened her.

'Sure, there's no harm to her,' Mother had assured the children when they were small. 'She gave your grandfather a rare gift, one time.' What the gift was, they were never told; nor did they ask. They hid themselves away whenever Meg — with her strange face, half-ugly, half-beautiful — came to the door. She offered to sell clothes-pegs whittled from hazel sticks, or hand-woven willow baskets. Sometimes she would merely ask for 'a sup o' tea to warm the pot'. Mother gave her it gladly, adding a thick slice of bread and jam for good measure, and chatted to her about the happenings of the countryside.

Aunt Mary was less generous. She kept her door firmly shut when Frosty Meg was around. 'That woman is untrustworthy,' was her opinion. 'She knows too much.'

What did Frosty Meg know? wondered Bridget as she sidled by. And why was she here so early in the year? True to her name, Frosty Meg was usually a winter visitor. Like the wild geese that came to the estuary (in smaller numbers now that the Factory was there), she never arrived in the area until autumn had set in.

The travelling woman paid Bridget no heed. Crouched in the road, surrounded by her bags and bundles, she was gazing at something cradled in her hands. Sneaking a look, Bridget saw it was a dead bird — a baby thrush with a brightly speckled breast, still young enough to have the fledgling's buttercup-yellow markings round its bill. For one startled moment she wondered if Frosty Meg had killed it, but she decided that couldn't be the case. There was a great tenderness in the way she smoothed its rumpled feathers. She was crooning softly in a language Bridget didn't know.

So many dead birds had been found recently, Bridget recalled as she went on her way. Not just farmers' hens, but wild birds, too, fallen from the trees and hedges like the unseasonably wilting leaves.

Lost in sad thought, Bridget didn't notice that she was walking down the middle of the road. Nor did she hear the car drawing up behind her — until it sounded its horn.

Bridget jumped hastily aside. The horn had a husky, well-oiled sound, like the voice of a very rich gentleman in the habit of wining and dining well. The car itself was just as grand: it was long, and black, and shiny enough to see your face in. It had tinted glass in its windscreen and side windows, and there was a silver mascot — a bird of prey — on its bonnet.

Michael, no doubt, would have been very impressed, and would have known the car's make and the exact year it had been built. All Bridget could do was stand and stare.

Sliding level with her, the limousine purred to a halt. The driver was a smart-liveried chauffeur. He sat straight and severe behind his steering-wheel, un-moving, eyes fixed on the road. He looked more like a part of the car than like a man. He ignored Bridget.

After a short interval, as if on its own, a back window slid down and a gloved hand was revealed. ('Gloves! At this time of year!' Bridget couldn't help thinking.) The hand beckoned.

Stupidly, Bridget glanced over her shoulder to see if she was the one being summoned. As there was no one else about, she supposed she must be. Timidly, she approached the car.

The interior was dim. It smelt of real leather and something else — something that caught at Bridget's throat and made her want to cough. The man's hair oil, perhaps? Or his expensive aftershave? Then why should she be reminded of the odours from the Factory?

As for the man himself, it was hard to make him out in the general gloom cast by the tinted windows. Bridget got the impression of a dark body hunched like a roosting bird against the smart upholstery, one elegantly gloved hand fiddling with an ivory-topped cane while the other plucked fretfully at the tartan rug across his knees.

'Manutronics Incorporated?' he enquired. His voice

was strange, half-croaky, half-sibilant. The 's' hissed like steam.

Bridget made no attempt to answer.

'Manutronics Incorporated?' The owner of the car became impatient. He leaned forward so that his face was framed in the open window. Hurriedly, Bridget stepped back. In spite of his smart clothes and accessories, his carefully sleeked-back hair and neatly trimmed moustache and beard, there was something about the man's face that spoke of terrible neglect. His cheeks were sunken and pale, almost the same colour as the ivory of his cane; his skin was pockmarked and stretched tight across the bones.

'He's rotting away,' Bridget thought. 'If it wasn't for all this' — her eyes took in the car, clothes, cane, chauffeur — 'he'd just crumble.' She was thankful she couldn't see the man's eyes — they were hidden by dark glasses — but she imagined them to be red-rimmed and watery. The stench in the car was getting worse.

'Th-that way,' she managed to stammer, pointing along the road towards the Factory.

The stranger seemed satisfied. Leaning back against the rich upholstery, he let out his breath with another hiss.

'Drive on,' he commanded the chauffeur, tapping him sharply on the shoulder with his cane. The window rolled up and the limousine purred off, leaving Bridget at first numb, then with her thoughts racing.

The croaking voice ... the hiss of breath ... the darkly humped body ....

'Why does he remind me of the crow?' she wondered.

Along the Green Road

*T*he man in the black limousine was the chief topic of conversation in Reilly's pub that night. Everyone, it seemed, had seen him — or, if they hadn't, they pretended they had. Rumours spread through the room. Customers drank uneasily. There was much talk of a visit from the big boss of the Factory, and of change.

'Sure, we've all been changed as it is, so what's different?' demanded the Logman, casting a black look at a group of intruders from the Factory who had stopped off to celebrate a raise in their salaries. In the centre of the group, loudest and merriest of all, was the children's Uncle Sean.

'That's true. And not for the better.' Bob stared gloomily into his half-empty glass.

'That was a great car he had,' remarked Shay Toomey, who hadn't seen it. 'A BMW, was it?'

If he received an answer he didn't hear it, for at that moment all conversation was drowned by a wave of shrieks and jeers from the pool room. Capped heads turned in disapproval.

'There's women there, too,' snorted the Logman (a prejudiced bachelor). 'Secretaries, in short skirts and make-up.'

'I used to love a game of the darts,' Bob mourned — the dartboard was surrounded by a circle of incomers too.

'The pair of you talk as if your lives were at an end,'

a younger man, Ted Fenton, teased. 'Come on, now. Tell us about the big shot today. Why is he here? What is he up to?'

The six locals, seated on wooden settles at their customary table in the corner, were the Logman and Bob; their friend Shay Toomey, a wind-wizened ex-fisherman; the two Fenton brothers, Ted and Frankie; and 'Fiddler' O'Sullivan, whose fiddle lay idle beside him — few people nowadays asked him to play. Beyond them, on the far side of a wooden partition with a hatch, Frosty Meg sat alone by the fire, nursing a pint of porter and crooning. The men were aware of her presence, but paid her no heed. While she was about she became part of the furniture.

'They say the Factory will more than double in size,' Frankie Fenton ventured. 'It's going to become an off-shoot of some great conglomerate in Europe. The boss is a Frenchman.'

'Is that so? I heard he was German.'

'A Dutchman, surely?'

'Whatever he is, he's foreign,' the Logman stated. 'Who but a foreigner would wear a beard and them gloves?' Getting up, he went to buy a pint of Guinness for his jennet.

'If the Factory grows any bigger, you can say good-bye to the fishing for ever,' Shay said. 'The river's polluted. All they're catching now is pinkeens, and they're deformed.'

'What we need is a partition,' Bob said emphatically, thumping his glass.

Puzzled, they stared at him. 'Like the Berlin Wall? I thought they'd demolished it.'

'A second border, maybe?'

'He means a *petition*,' the Fiddler said (as a travelling musician he had seen some of the world). 'One of them long lists of names to show to the Government.'

They began to count heads. Even including the Logman, who was still at the bar, their list was too short.

'What did the Government ever do for us, anyway?' Shay Toomey asked bitterly.

'That Sean Foley is drinking large whiskeys, and buying the rounds,' the Logman announced as he returned.

'And why wouldn't he? Hasn't he just been promoted?' They all glared at the traitor.

'Why has the other brother gone to America?' Frankie was curious.

'Mind your own business,' the Logman snapped.

Bob considered the matter. As 'stand-in' at the farm, he should be in the know.

'Hard to tell,' he said. 'There seems to have been some sort of disagreement ....'

'Between the two brothers?'

He didn't answer.

'It's that wife of Sean's,' the Fiddler suggested. 'She's over-ambitious.'

'That's true.' They all nodded.

'Weren't the two brothers always as different as fish and fowl, anyway?' Shay Toomey said. 'Always quarrelling. Just like their father, old Seamus, and his brother before them. Perhaps it's as well the next generation is one of each — a boy and a girl.' He turned to the Logman. 'You've known the Foleys this long time. What do you say?'

The Logman considered his glass (and the jennet's). 'I'll say only one thing,' he replied, 'and it's this: if my old friend Seamus hadn't gone missing that time, leaving his no-good brother John in charge of the farm, things would have been different. There would have been no Factory. And nothing for his two sons to fight over.' He tossed back his head and emptied his glass.

This was too mysterious — too difficult to understand. Eagerly, they leant forward, hoping to learn more. They all knew something about old Seamus's strange disappearance, many years before. No one knew quite where he'd gone, or why. There had been a woman involved, they'd been told, and there had been a great quarrel between the two brothers when Seamus returned. Following the quarrel, the farm had shrunk in size; some said John had sold land behind Seamus's back. Then John had emigrated to America, and nothing had been heard of him since.

Silence reigned. Expectations were high. On the far side of the wooden partition screening the group from the fire, Frosty Meg put down her porter. She stopped crooning. She sat alert, listening.

They were in for a disappointment. 'Well, I'm off. I'll bid you good night.' The Logman rose to his feet. Taking up his jennet's drink, he made for the door.

After a few seconds, Frosty Meg drained her glass. She left her place by the fire and followed him.

'That was a deal of gossip,' she remarked, when she got outside. 'You were the worst of them all. Have you got no more sense? You should keep your knowledge for the trees.'

The Logman grunted. He concentrated on offering the Guinness to the jennet, tied to a lamppost near the door. He resented criticism, especially from a woman, and most especially from Frosty Meg; he had an old grudge against her.

'Lured him away, that's what you did,' he growled. 'And what use was your gift, after all?'

'The story's not told yet,' Frosty Meg countered.

The Logman glowered. 'Don't you go meddling,' he

snapped. 'Your meddling's not needed. Things are bad enough as it is.'

'It could be my meddling is just what's needed,' Frosty Meg remarked tartly. Gathering her colourful rags around her, she dug behind the dustbins, where she had hidden her bags and bundles before entering the pub. No one had touched them; they looked too much like part of the rubbish. Knowing their owner, no one would have dared touch them anyway.

'Good night to you,' she said, stringing her possessions around her. Patting the jennet's neck, she sailed off, a bright ship in the moonlight.

'Good night,' the Logman said grudgingly, in case she ill-wished him. He busied himself with the straps on the jennet's harness and didn't watch her go.

Bundles swinging and swaying around her, Frosty Meg swept through the moonshine and out of the town. Once in the countryside, her way was criss-crossed by branches — some leafy, some not.

At the Foleys' farmstead, she came to a halt. Beyond the wall, a calf bawled in the barn; nearby, a cow, half-asleep but still missing its youngster, moaned softly. There was no Grip, now, to warn people of the traveller's presence; there was just Timkit, golden-eyed in the moonlight on top of the wall.

Frosty Meg looked at the cat. 'You're putting on weight,' she observed critically. 'What you want is a strict diet and plenty of exercise. I'm thinking you'll be getting it soon.' She leaned on the gate.

The yard was half lit, half in shadow. High up, a beam from an attic window (Bridget's) spread over the tiles and into Grandfather's tree. Where it landed, the branch was bare and shrivelled. A piece of plastic flapped dismally. Underneath, there were leaves on the ground.

Frosty Meg shuddered. 'You can tell *he's* been here,' she said to herself.

Letting her bundles fall, she hoisted up her skirts and hopped over the gate. Bending over, she gathered up the fallen leaves.

'Time to start meddling,' she announced, stowing the fragile objects in the pockets of her voluminous skirts and straightening her back. 'Fetch your mistress,' she told Timkit. 'Be quick, now. Follow me.'

She hopped back over the gate, retrieved her bundles, and went on her way.

Timkit watched her, unblinking. After she had gone, he rose to his feet and yawned hugely. 'Fat, is it?' he was thinking, hackles raised. 'We shall see!'

He stretched all four legs, one after the other, and shook every paw. When he was ready, with surprising agility for such a plump cat, he sprang from the wall to the tree and up through its branches. Alighting on Bridget's windowsill, he opened his mouth and caterwauled.

There was no reply. Timkit yowled again, louder.

'Timkit! Whatever's the matter?' Bridget was still up and dressed. She had extra homework to do after Sister Moira's lecture at school. She flung open the window. She had been missing her nightly companion; he had gone straight out after supper and hadn't returned. Calling had been useless, and asking her family had led nowhere; Michael wasn't interested, and Mother was busy with Grandfather, who wasn't feeling well.

Bridget expected Timkit to leap from the windowsill into the room, but he didn't. Instead, he mewed twice and scampered back down the tree to stand at the bottom. His eyes glinted as they stared up at her. He opened his mouth. He was mewing again.

'Really, Timkit! You are a nuisance,' Bridget said,

exasperated. 'I suppose you think I'm coming all the way down to carry you upstairs?'

The cat mewed once more, pitifully.

Grumbling, Bridget closed her books and stamped downstairs. There was nobody in the kitchen; the fire had gone low. She could hear Mother talking to Grandfather in his bedroom next door.

When she opened the back door, Timkit began to behave very strangely. As she had expected, he wove himself round her legs, purring loudly; but he refused to come in. When she tried to pick him up, he wriggled free and went to stand by the gate. Looking back, he gave a miaow.

'All right. Have it your own way.' Bridget started to shut the back door. Immediately Timkit was at her feet again, weaving figures of eight round her ankles, gazing up into her eyes.

Bridget stared at the cat. She had never known him to act like this. He was behaving the way old Grip had when he wanted a walk. Leaping to the gatepost, he was looking over his shoulder and waving his tail. It was plain that he wanted her to follow.

Puzzled, Bridget fetched her blazer from the hook on the door. Glancing round the kitchen, she saw a bowl of apples on the table and put two in her pockets.

For a moment she hesitated. In the old days, she would have run upstairs to get Michael to share the adventure. But since he had acquired a catapult and a gang of rough friends, things were different. Instead she slipped out alone, quietly closing the door.

Timkit greeted her with enthusiasm, purring and responding to her stroking before leaping down and starting along the road. Bridget followed him.

They travelled with their backs to the town. All was quiet. No cars passed them by. A gentle night breeze teased the hedgerows, and from the grass verge of the ditch came the faint rustlings of small creatures busy with their night-time pursuits. Once a barn owl flew overhead, silent and ghostly. Timkit neither paused nor looked back. With his tail-tip twitching (was he beckoning?) he picked his way purposefully down the road.

They passed by houses and farms Bridget knew; there were lights in some of the windows, but they saw no one. The fields became scarce, the land wild and untamed, as they drew nearer the hills.

Bridget began to feel frightened. It was late. Surely it was time to go home? They'd get lost. She tried calling the cat's name (not too loudly; she was afraid someone might hear), but Timkit didn't respond. Without even looking round, he kept walking, just a few yards ahead.

As if in a dream, they went on. Not a soul passed them by, but every now and then Bridget thought she could see a figure moving in front of them.

'Just a trick of the moonlight,' she assured herself; for each time, before her eyes became certain of what they were seeing, the figure vanished, swallowed up by a shadow or hidden by a bend in the road.

By now the hills were quite close. They looked much higher and steeper than they seemed from the farm. The road wound uphill. On either side, the wind whipped the heather. Bridget felt chilly in her thin school blazer, and she was becoming footsore.

'I really must turn back,' she decided. 'If Timkit won't come, it's his problem.'

She had scarcely said this when the cat came to a sudden halt. He sat down on the road.

At last! Bridget caught up with him. Now was the time to persuade him to turn back; he was miles from his hunting-grounds.

Timkit sat still and ignored her. His whiskers twitched. His eyes, green globes in the moonlight, stared straight at the hills.

This was too much! Bridget lost all patience. Bending, she scooped him up in her arms. Timkit was no light-weight, but if she had to carry him all the way home, she decided, she would!

She had barely taken a step when a voice spoke nearby.

'And where do you think you're going?' it asked. 'Having come this far, shouldn't you finish the journey?'

Bridget dropped the cat. Her heart in her mouth, she turned round.

A figure was emerging from a turf clump by the side of the road — a woman .... Frosty Meg! The moonlight glinted on the earrings she wore and picked out patterns of yellow and blue on her clothing.

All Bridget wanted to do was turn and run, but Timkit had other ideas. Hurt in his paws and his dignity by his drop to the road, he went to Frosty Meg. Bridget had no choice but to follow. Timkit had behaved oddly all night; now, she decided, watching the way he was treating Frosty Meg like an old friend, he was being disloyal.

'What kept you? I thought you'd never catch up.' Frosty Meg addressed her remarks to the cat. Brushing turf-dust and cat-hairs from her skirts, she picked up her belongings. In the moonlight she looked unusually tall — more than six feet. By contrast, Timkit's stubby, marmalade-striped figure seemed tiny.

Hesitantly, Bridget moved round so that she could see the beautiful side of the travelling woman's face rather than the ugly side. Strangely, she was beginning to lose her fear, and she wanted to ask Frosty Meg what she had meant by the word 'journey'.

She was given no chance. Beyond the woman's tall frame, a green road wound ribbon-like through the heather. Already Frosty Meg had turned and, long skirts flapping about her ankles, was striding along it. Timkit bounded, his tail straight like a kitten's, and overtook her.

Again, Bridget was left with no choice. She ran after them.

'Where are we going?' she pleaded breathlessly as she caught up.

Frosty Meg made no reply. She increased her pace. Beneath their feet, the grass felt soft as a mattress. Beside them, their shadows danced jigs over the heather ....

Before them, the green road stretched away to the hills.

Passcard to Another World

*M*ichael was feeling neglected. He had awoken
that morning to a stillness which suggested there
was no one about. He missed the usual knock at the
door and his mother's voice reminding him that it was
late and he had better get up. Things were unnaturally
quiet in Bridget's bedroom next door. He checked his
watch to make sure he hadn't made a mistake and
woken too early. It was a quarter to eight.

'Strange! It's like being the only survivor of a nuclear
holocaust,' Michael thought. As he had a lively imagination, fed by the comics he read and the programmes
he watched on TV, he was happy to lie back for a while,
wondering how long he would have to remain in an
airtight capsule (as, unlike Bridget, he never opened
his window at night, that was almost true!) and where
he could find uncontaminated food and water.

The thought of food, contaminated or otherwise,
reminded him of breakfast. By now it was eight
o'clock, and he was hungry — and bored!

Reaching over, he thumped on the wall. 'Bridget!
What are you doing?' he asked fretfully.

There was no answer.

'Snob! I don't talk to girls, anyway.' Nevertheless,
once Michael was dressed, he went and banged on her
door. Not a sound. 'I suppose Miss Prim-and-Perfect
has been up for hours,' he thought.

'This is a police raid!' he announced loudly. Putting his hand to the doorknob and his shoulder to the panel, he burst in.

To his surprise, the room was empty, and looked as if it had been so all night. Bridget's schoolbooks were still on her desk, where she had left them. Her bed hadn't been slept in. Mystified, and not a little alarmed, Michael withdrew.

Downstairs, matters were no better. Everything looked unusually neat and clean, as if it had been swept by a new broom. The fire flickered primly in a well-polished grate. There was no Mother, humming cheerfully to herself as she prepared breakfast; there was just Aunt Mary, presiding over an expertly laid table.

'Your grandfather has had another slight stroke,' she informed Michael, with a smug I-knew-this-would-happen tone to her voice. 'Nothing to worry about, I'm sure, but your mother has gone with him to the hospital. I'm here to help. Eat your breakfast. Where's Bridget?'

Michael opened his mouth to say that Bridget wasn't in her room and he didn't know where she was, but then he thought better of it. Whatever Bridget was up to, he was quite sure she didn't want Aunt Mary to know. In a time-honoured habit left over from the past, when they had been better friends and had shared all their secrets, he lied.

'Bridget got up very early today, Aunty Mary,' he said, with his most wide-eyed innocent look (wasted — she had turned away from him). 'She's gone off to school already. She had an important project to finish.'

If Aunt Mary thought this was strange, she didn't say so. She merely repeated her instruction to eat breakfast, and busied herself rearranging the kitchen.

'But it's cornflakes. I hate cornflakes.' Michael wrinkled his nose. 'Can't I have toast?'

'You'll eat what's provided,' his aunt told him.

Michael toyed with his cornflakes. Behind his aunt's back, he made himself a thick bread-and-marmalade sandwich and stuffed it into his pocket for later. Without another word, he fetched his school-bag and catapult and let himself out through the back door.

'Did you see Bridget?' he asked Bob, who was hosing the haggard.

'I did not. Mind yourself!' Bob was not in a good mood; he had lingered too long in Reilly's the night before. 'I suppose hell will freeze before that one brings me a cup of tea,' he grumbled, nodding towards the house.

Michael shrugged. He crossed to Grandfather's tree.

There were a great many more leaves on the ground, which showed that Bridget hadn't been by to pick them up. Feeling foolish, aware of his aunt's eye upon him from the window, Michael picked them up for her. Not knowing what else to do, he shoved them into his pocket, on top of the marmalade sandwich.

He was late for school anyway, so he decided to play truant. Making sure that no one was watching, he turned down the road that led to the river. Despite himself, he was worried about Bridget. It wasn't like her to disappear without telling anyone where she was going.

'Maybe she's been captured by pirates,' Michael thought, aiming a stone at a telegraph pole (he missed it). 'Or the Mafia! Or Soviet agents! Or space travellers!'

He was so busy with plans to rescue his sister (who would be eternally grateful to him, of course, and indebted to him forever) that he didn't notice he had taken the wrong fork in the road. Instead of coming to the river shore, where he had planned to turn over stones looking for winkles, he had ended up further downstream, where the river widened and grew silty, and the Factory, crouched on its concrete platform, spewed its brew of leftovers into the mud. A lost brook, choked with garbage, seeped sulkily through what had once been water-meadows, and under a bridge. Across the bridge the road widened, leading straight to the Factory gates. No winkles there!

Michael was about to turn back when he noticed a large black limousine parked on the bridge. Beside it, a smart-liveried chauffeur lounged against the parapet, smoking a cigarette.

'That's the car the fellows at school were on about,' Michael thought, edging closer. There was something about the chauffeur's face and his way of standing that suggested he would not like to be questioned by a small boy, nor would he be flattered by having his car admired. So, before reaching the bridge, Michael dodged aside and slipped over a low wall. Ducking down, he followed the bank of the brook to a place where he could study the car without being seen. Using his school-bag to give himself extra height, supporting himself with the tips of his fingers on the concrete parapet of the bridge, he managed to get a good view. Beyond the car's glossy paintwork, blue smoke from the chauffeur's cigarette curled lazily upwards.

'Vehicle in question now under surveillance,' Michael reported in his mind to an imaginary radio hidden upon his person. 'Black BMW — no, correction: Mercedes. Model unknown. Mascot on bonnet: a bird of prey with outstretched wings. Registration number ....'

He was easing his way along, trying to get a glimpse of the car's number-plate (if it was a personalised one, it might give him a clue about its owner), when a sudden hubbub of voices from the Factory compound almost made him tumble off his perch.

The great gates burst open and a crowd streamed through.

'What's happening? Is it a strike? A revolution?' Excitement kept Michael in place. Teetering violently on the sagging school-bag, he managed to cling to the bridge, his neck craned towards the Factory.

Not a revolution, he concluded disappointedly; all the people were too well-dressed. Smart-suited men with highly polished shoes and executive briefcases were tripping over their own feet in an effort to keep up. They were trailed by female secretaries hobbled by short skirts, high heels, and a duty to make notes.

The leader and chief attraction of this band, drawing the smartly dressed executives behind him like a magnet collecting pins, was a tall, thin, bearded, foreign-looking gentleman in an immaculate black overcoat, dark glasses, and gloves. He walked with authority, swinging an ivory-topped cane.

Coming to a halt so abruptly that the people behind cannoned into one another trying to avoid him, he swung round to face the crowd. Silence fell. Faces took on a look of earnest concentration. Secretaries stood to attention, notebooks prepared.

'The decision is made,' the stranger hissed into the silence. There was something about his voice that made Michael's red hair stand on end. 'There is no need for the public to know. I cannot emphasise this too strongly. There must be no questions in the Dáil, no publicity. You understand? Tracey! The car.'

The chauffeur jerked into action. He flung the cigarette, still alight, over the parapet. It narrowly missed Michael, and it made him fall off his school-bag.

Landing in the mud, he heard the car door slam and the vehicle reverse, turn, and purr away. After a short interval of subdued silence, the hubbub broke out again, growing fainter as the managers and their followers disappeared behind the Factory gates.

Cold mud seeping through his trouser legs, Michael watched the cigarette glow, then burn itself out. The stranger's voice was still hissing in his head, making his flesh creep.

When at last his trousers became too uncomfortably wet and soggy, he stirred. Nearby, something else had fallen in the mud. Crawling over on hands and knees, he picked it up and took it to a drier part of the bank, where he could examine it in detail.

It was a laminated plastic card, like the one Uncle Sean carried when he went to work; but this one was particularly black and shiny and rich-looking, and it had silver letters and numbers stamped on it. The letters and numbers made no sense. They were in a weird, angular script that Michael didn't recognise. Above them was a logo, only visible if you twisted the card from side to side. One way it seemed to be a tree with bare branches; the other, it was a volcano spurting lava. A tiny, but unmistakable, bird of prey hovered on minuscule wings above the main design.

'Might come in useful, I suppose.' Michael gave the card a wipe on the cleaner part of his trousers. He had visions of himself sauntering up to the Factory gates one day, presenting the card and being admitted — 'As a sort of undercover agent,' he imagined, stowing it in his only free pocket, where it slid down amongst the marbles. 'Industrial espionage!'

All this had put thoughts of Bridget quite out of his mind. It was too early to treat himself to a picnic of his marmalade sandwich, especially as it was all the food he was likely to get that day, so he decided to follow the brook to its source. It was hardly the Amazon, but if he was lucky he might find a few adventures along the way. He hid his school-bag under the parapet of the bridge so as not to have to carry it around, and, catapult at the ready, began his journey.

Once free of the Factory, the brook lost its dead look and became quite lively, slipping through the fields and burbling happily over the stones, unaware of what would happen when it reached the estuary. Watched only by a handful of bullocks and a few sheep, Michael made his way upstream. Every now and then he aimed his catapult at a bush growing on the bank, on the off-chance that it might contain a jaguar or a desperate savage armed with poisoned arrows. A half-submerged log became a mighty alligator; he fought for a while with an anaconda in the shape of a tangle of ivy, using stones from the brook rather than waste his supply of marbles.

Normally, these delights of the imagination would have kept him in one spot for most of the morning; but for some reason, since he had put the passcard in his pocket Michael was becoming increasingly restless. The game of 'going up the Amazon' began to pall. Instead, he took to seeing how many stones he could jump on without getting his feet wet. After falling in the water five times, he lost interest in this game too.

'Stupid thing!' he said, giving the last stone a kick and stubbing his toes. Thrusting his hands into his pockets, he trudged gloomily along, feeling that some-how the morning had been spoilt and he might have been better off going to school after all.

He soon found that putting his hands in his pockets was a mistake, too. He had forgotten what was in them. In no time one hand was all covered in marmalade, with clusters of silver leaves sticking to it; as for the other, he cut his finger on the sharp edge of the plastic card.

The cut was more painful than it should have been. Angrily, Michael snatched his hands from his pockets. Blood dripped on the grass. Wiping his marmaladey hand on the bank, he searched for a handkerchief, but it was the one thing his pockets didn't contain. The best he could do was make a sort of poultice with the marmalade and leaves. This worked surprisingly well; the bleeding stopped.

'I've invented a new medicine,' Michael thought, and continued on his way in better spirits.

The end of the journey, however, was a disappointment.

A very ordinary metal pipe was draining water from a small hill into a sunken cattle trough, where it trickled out to give rise to the beginnings of the brook. All around, the ground was messy and cut up by the feet of cows. So much for great cascades, hidden wells, water bubbling from a mystic source!

'Oh, well — if the cattle can drink here, I suppose it's all right for me too,' Michael told himself. He was thirsty. He had the sense to avoid the trough. He bent towards the pipe; but as he did so, he was sure he heard someone calling, deep down inside the hill. Was that Bridget's voice?

Suddenly remembering his sister's absence at breakfast, Michael jerked upright, staring at the drain. Was it possible? Was she stuck inside? The pipe did seem wider than he had thought at first. Dramatic headlines flashed across Michael's brain: '*Courageous Boy Rescues Sister Trapped in Drain!*' Cautiously, he stepped onto the rim of the trough and peered into the dark.

As he did so, the passcard in his pocket gave a lurch

and flicked over on its side. Michael heard a slight click, as if some electronic mechanism was being activated. The pipe widened visibly, and, to his horror, Michael was drawn inside.

Water spurting against his face, spluttering and gasping, he plunged downward at a sickening rate — to land with a splash in a deep, dark pool. With bursting lungs, he sank beneath the icy surface — down, down, down ... until he reached the bottom. As his feet touched something solid, he became aware of lights flashing and mocking voices sounding in his ears. Taking this for a sign that he was drowning, he fought his way upwards.

He gulped air, sank again, and finally resurfaced — only to find that the lights and voices were no illusion.

All around the pool flamed a circle of fiery torches, shooting darts of light across the ripples and making grotesque shadows shudder and leap up the walls of a cavern. The torches were held in the hands of the most peculiar and hideous creatures Michael had ever known. They were part-man, part-bird; half-black, half-white. They were hopping and jumping at the edge of the water, running to and fro in a frenzy, pointing at him with bony fingers. He could understand only one word of their jabbering speech: 'Card! Card! Card!' uttered in the raucous cry of magpies.

Despite the weight of water upon it, the passcard in his pocket gave another lurch. Realising it might be his only means of rescue, Michael managed to fish it out.

Treading water to prevent himself from sinking, he lifted it high and held it out to the weird black-and-white bird-men on the bank.

A Bridge of Mist

"*W*e can't go in there!' objected Bridget.

The cave in the heart of the hill looked black and forbidding, especially now that the moon was half-masked by a bank of cloud. Perched on a rock, she looked at its gap-toothed entrance apprehensively. The rock she was sitting on was spongy with damp moss; dripping clusters of hart's-tongue fern lapped her ankles. From somewhere close by in the darkness came the never-ending sound of rushing water.

Frosty Meg made no reply. She was using this pause in their journey to remove her boots, tie the laces together, and add them to the string of her other belongings. This done, she rose to her feet and moved away in the direction of the hidden stream. They had reached the end of the green road. And they had lost Timkit!

Sliding off the rock, Bridget tried calling once again: 'Timmy! Timmy! Tim, Tim, Tim!' Her heart wasn't in her cries. She guessed where the cat had gone. Despite his natural dislike of water, he had leapt the torrent and vanished into the craggy opening in the hillside.

Was there ever such a contrary cat? Moon-madness — that was what was wrong with him. And it was affecting this strange, silent woman who was insisting on leading them on some sort of 'journey'. 'It's infected me, too,' Bridget thought grimly. 'I should have been in bed hours ago. I still haven't finished my homework.'

Taking off her shoes and socks, she struggled across the turbulent stream after Frosty Meg. For some reason she didn't understand, she left her shoes — with her socks, neatly rolled, inside them — side by side at the mouth of the cave, and entered barefoot.

Frosty Meg was waiting for her. Without a word, she placed a hand on Bridget's shoulder and guided her into the dark.

And it certainly was dark! Bridget tested each step with nervous toes. The blackness swallowed her up like soup. Soon, her only connections with reality were the hard, cold stone beneath her bare feet and the travelling woman's firm hand at her back — and the ever-present fear that she would walk straight into the rocky wall!

'It's all very well for Timkit,' she said to herself sourly. 'Cats can see in the dark.' It crossed her mind that the woman behind her might have cat's eyes, too, for there was no hesitancy in the way she moved.

Step by tentative step, Bridget crept forward. In the darkness it was impossible to tell whether the cave was broad or narrow, high or low. Certainly, it was high enough that she didn't bump her head against the roof. There could be no doubt that it was long and deep.

Time lost all meaning. The air they breathed felt stuffy, stale, as if it had been trapped underground for centuries and most of the oxygen had been worn away. Occasionally, relief came in the form of an icy blast blown from — where?

Were they going north? south? east? west? Like time, direction served no purpose. Sometimes Bridget got the impression that they were standing still; at other times, she thought they were spiralling round and round. Just as she grew dizzy, the way would straighten, and Frosty Meg would hurry her along with a firm push on her shoulder-blades.

At least the cave was dry, Bridget thought thankfully; and the floor was smooth, so once she got used to it there was no fear of tripping. 'The cave must have been worn through the rock by the stream outside,' she supposed, 'long ago, before the water changed its course.'

She kept her mind on these things because she didn't want to dwell on what they might meet in the dark depths. Bats lived in caves, she knew; and spiders. There could be other creatures, long and slimy ....

For some time, they had been travelling upwards. Bridget couldn't be certain, but she felt the blackness was growing less intense. A welcome breeze, soft and warm and bearing a scent of herbs, blew in their faces. Presently, a pinprick of light that had been playing peek-a-boo grew larger; it swelled to the size of a tennis ball, a hoop, a big round 'O' .... And framed within it — surely that heap of fur was cat-shaped? It had pricked ears, whiskers, a long twitching tail ....

Breaking loose from Frosty Meg's restraining hands, Bridget dashed forward. To her surprise and joy, she burst out into broad daylight.

She fell to her knees on a grassy hillside. All around her, the ground was speckled with bright flowers; larks sang in a clear blue sky, butterflies danced on rainbow wings, rabbits bobbed fearlessly, trees rustled in a gentle breeze. And all was reflected in the still waters of a lake laid out like a mirror at the foot of the slope.

And there sat Timkit, pleased as punch, in the flowery grass, overflowing with pride and purrs. 'Look what I've found,' his attitude seemed to say. 'Tell me, now: aren't I the clever one?'

'Oh, you are. You are!' Bridget hugged him until he

scratched and spat. 'You're the cleverest cat in the world!'

'I wouldn't say that,' said Frosty Meg, coming up behind her. 'You went too fast,' she lectured the cat. 'Now we're early; we'll have to wait.' Grumbling, she marched to the shore of the lake, dumped her bundles, and sat on them. Producing a clay pipe from a pocket, she filled it from a small linen pouch, lit up, and started to smoke.

Bridget was dying to ask what they were waiting for. But by now she had given up all hope of having her questions answered. And as it was such a pleasant spot to linger in anyway, especially after the long, suffocating hours in the cave (had they been in there all night? she wondered), she sat down on the grass beside Frosty Meg.

They waited for what seemed like an age. Hunched over her pipe, Frosty Meg watched the lake. The smoke didn't smell like tobacco; rather, it was a mix of — hawthorn flowers? wild thyme? water mint? the nutty scent of gorse-buds on a sunny hillside? Growing bored, Timkit stretched and moved off to paw at the dragonflies hanging like jewels round the yellow irises at the water's margin. A group of swans appeared from the bulrushes further down the shore and sailed towards them, their black feet sending ripples to either side. The breeze ruffled their white feathers as they came. One, two, three, four — one for each of the Children of Lir! Bridget half-expected them to speak to her in human voices, but they merely bowed their stately heads as they swam past. Hidden in mist on the far side of the lake, a curlew called plaintively. Frosty Meg cocked her head and listened.

Bursting with unanswered questions and unable to restrain herself any longer, Bridget chose just one. 'Where are we?' she demanded.

Frosty Meg didn't even bother to look at her. 'About halfway.'

'Halfway to where?'

The travelling woman removed her pipe from her mouth. The face she turned towards Bridget was startling in its contrast: one side was twisted and grotesque, the other almost ethereally beautiful.

'The Land Beyond,' she said.

'Oh!' Grandfather's face swam before Bridget's eyes — younger, healthier; full of mischief, as it had always been. Light played upon it, cast by the moving branches of the silver tree .... 'Where did the tree come from, Grandfather?' she had asked. 'The land beyond,' he had replied ....

Restlessly, she rose to her feet and tried to peer across the water. It was no use; the far shore was hidden by a band of mist.

'Hadn't we better get going?' she asked uneasily. Judging by the stretch of water to either side, the lake would take them many hours to walk round. They had wasted time already.

'No. Wait.' Frosty Meg's hand reached up and pulled her back. 'Magic builds slowly. It can't be rushed,' she said mysteriously. And she went back to smoking her pipe.

They sat in silence. Frosty Meg continued to puff at her pipe, occasionally taking the stem from her mouth to blow smoke far out across the water. On the far side of the lake the mist continued to gather, a high, white wall. The swans swam back the way they had come, bending their heads once more as if in greeting. Once more, the curlew called. Weary of trying to catch the uncatchable, Timkit came and curled up on Bridget's knee. Idly, she stroked him, her eyes following the twisting skeins of smoke above the water.

Suddenly she stiffened, her fingers pinching Timkit's skin so that he mewed and dug in his claws in protest. Something was happening on the far side of the lake!

The wall of mist was lifting, rising like a curtain in the theatre to reveal the scene behind. Once in the sky, its vapours swirled and bunched and gathered, hanging in great swathes.

The travelling woman smiled, one corner of her mouth crooked, the other spreading like a charm. Taking the pipe from between her lips, she blew a final puff of smoke across the water. Immediately, small eddies of air rushed to collect it, bearing it and the other curlicues of smoke away to fill the space the mist had left. Reaching the mist, the smoke began to cling and mingle, twisting and teasing the white vapours as if they were tufts of wool, spinning each strand and drawing it out tight before weaving away — weft over warp — to form a ....

Bridget sprang to her feet. Clutching the cat, she ran down to the water's edge. Tiny wavelets sucked at her bare toes, but she took no notice.

Across the water lay the Land Beyond — mountain and forest, meadow and stream, all breathtakingly beautiful, bathed in golden light. And above her head rose the great pylons and shimmering arch of a bridge! It spanned the lake from shore to shore.

'Ahhh!' Frosty Meg let out a long sigh of satisfaction at a job well done. 'Just what are we waiting for?' she demanded, bending to knock her pipe out against a stone. 'For the thing to melt?'

She pocketed her pipe and advanced towards the bridge. 'Come along,' she called, laying her hand on the handrail. She started to walk across.

Bridget tore her eyes away from the shakings of Frosty Meg's pipe, which had grown into yellow flowers in the grass. 'You've forgotten your bags and bundles,' she called. Receiving no reply as usual, she gripped Timkit tightly and hurried after Frosty Meg.

She expected her feet to sink into the insubstantial surface of the bridge, but it felt surprisingly strong, and only dipped slightly when she stepped onto it. It was impossible to hold the handrail while controlling a struggling cat. Bridget went forward with extreme care, keeping her eyes on her feet.

At the summit of the arch, Frosty Meg came to a stop. 'This is as far as I go,' she announced. 'You'll be in other hands from now on.'

'But ....' Bridget stared at her, appalled. Whose hands did she mean, she wondered?

'I can't go on alone,' her mind was shouting, 'not with the magic and all. I don't even know why I'm here!' Now that they were standing still, she could feel the bridge swaying in the breeze. She suspected it might blow away at any minute.

'You're here to help,' Frosty Meg informed her, as if she had heard the unspoken protest. 'As for the details, you'll find them out as you go along. Now let's check you over.' Her eyes — kinder than usual — travelled from Bridget's head to her toes and back again. 'Barefoot. Quite right. It will give you a better grip on the Far Shore. Also, it means you've left something behind to draw you back home, which is even better. Have you anything to eat? It isn't wise to taste Their food.'

Bridget nodded dumbly, feeling for an apple.

'That's all right, then. Whatever you do, don't look back until you've left the bridge. One last thing: trust the cat. He may be fat and lazy, but his paw is sure. Goodbye, now. May luck go with you.'

'Help? How?'

There could be no argument. Frosty Meg gave

Bridget a push to send her on her way. Hugging Timkit to her chest, she unsteadily began to descend the span. Obediently, she didn't look back.

If she had, she might have seen a strange expression — half-hope, half-regret — on the travelling woman's face. 'Such troops!' Frosty Meg was saying to herself, as she watched the small, retreating figure — thin and fragile, but amazingly straight-backed in her school blazer — with the cat's ginger tail bobbing beneath her elbow. 'Such troops! All we have left to fight with. Will they be enough, I wonder?'

Frosty Meg rested for a moment on the parapet of the bridge, gazing down into the mirror-clear water as if into a fortune-teller's glass. The image she saw there alarmed her. 'What are they doing to him?' she demanded. 'The room so clean and lifeless, and him just lying there half-smothered in wires and tubes — it's a wonder he has any breath at all .... I'm coming, old man. I'm coming.'

She hurried back the way she had come: across the bridge, over the flowery grass, through the dark cave, and along the green road.

Still without looking back, Bridget continued to walk the last part of the bridge. Reaching the other side, she stepped down cautiously.

Once again the curlew was calling, nearer and louder than before. Somehow, heard from close by, it didn't sound quite like a bird ....

Bridget had scarcely taken one step when, with a spit and a snarl, Timkit leapt from her arms and streaked towards the nearest tree. There was a loud barking, and something hurtled towards her. The impact sent her reeling. Gasping, she hit the ground, landing flat on her back.

A large and very hairy dog was standing on her chest.

The Bird King's Fortress

*B*ony black-and-white fingers reached out towards Michael. He was grabbed by many hands and dragged this way and that across the rocks before being hoisted to the shore, where he was pinched and poked and the passcard was taken away. The magpie-men released him and went into a huddle. Their grating voices sank into whispers.

Still shivering and choking, Michael regarded the magpie-men with distaste. They seemed made up of bits and pieces and spare parts. Men's faces, wizened as monkeys' yet strangely childlike, had been forced like masks onto heads which, from the way they bobbed and cocked from side to side, must surely once have belonged to birds. Despite the false vivacity of these movements, the faces remained expressionless; they were all of one type, as if cast from the same crooked mould. As for their bodies, they were chalk-white and coal-black in patches, like a tinker's horse, and their skin was rough and pimply, as if their feathers had recently been plucked. Loose skin-flaps spreading between their protruding ribs and elbows, and the beginnings of webbing at the bases of their fingers, suggested wings; but it was obvious that these creatures never flew. Hopping, with their bony arms outstretched, would be the nearest they could come to such a joy.

Whatever else had gone into their manufacture, brains were obviously in short supply. It was clear, from the way they were peering and prodding at the card and quarrelling among themselves, that they couldn't read its message and didn't know what to do next. In collecting it from him, Michael guessed, they had been obeying some sort of command; now that they had it, they had no idea what should follow.

Taking a risk, he made the mistake of moving. At once, the magpie-men's mob instinct took over. With birdlike cries they pounced on him, their hands like claws.

Frantically breaking loose, Michael dashed for the only exit he could see from the rocky chamber. As he sprang over the threshold, he was aware of a loud rattling and grinding above his head. Whether it was a roof-fall, or whether he had triggered some mechanism which caused a great stone door to roll down, he would never know.

To his relief, he found himself outside the cavern — alone.

He leaned against the newly formed stone wall at his back, listening to the faint jabbering of the magpie-men on the other side and gazing along the gloomy corridor in which he found himself. Damp dripped from the ceiling and oozed down the walls in the form of slimy fungus. Here and there along the walls, fiery torches like those the magpie-men had held sputtered fretfully, threatening to fall from their rusting sconces.

However, Michael's relief didn't last long. It soon became painfully obvious that air was in short supply. His forehead was beginning to feel cold and clammy, his breathing laboured, his mind fuzzy at the edges. There was nothing to be done but follow the passage and hope it would lead him to fresher air.

Supporting himself on the slimy wall, he went along. The passage seemed endless. Chilly vapours wafted along it, lapping around his ankles like the ghosts of waves, hiding the floor so that he couldn't tell where to put his feet.

Nevertheless, gradually the air above the vapour became fresher; the torches, in their rusty sconces, burned more brightly. But they were no more secure; Michael jumped in alarm as one of them toppled suddenly and landed, with a hiss, just a yard from his toes. After that, to avoid being set alight, he walked down the centre of the passage, where there was a deeply worn groove which suggested the tramping of many feet — or the possibility that at one time the place had been flooded and a channel had been carved by rushing water.

As the vapour cleared, Michael noticed doors on either side of the passage, between the sconces. They were of solid wood or iron, set with high grilles. Most of the grilles were shuttered, and those that were left open were dark; but Michael felt sure he could hear shufflings and groans, and the occasional pathetic scratching noise, beyond the bars.

Then, to his horror, he heard one of the doors slamming far behind him, and the brisk *pad-pad-pad* of approaching feet.

He increased his pace. Had the magpie-men managed to break out of the cavern? Whoever it was couldn't help but hear him, for the passage echoed like a drum.

Not the magpie-men, he decided, as the feet increased their speed to match his own. This person was alone — but no less menacing for that. Stumbling along the uneven groove, Michael broke into a run.

At last, the end of the passage was in sight. A cluster of newly lit torches marked the spot ....

To Michael's dismay, they revealed yet another
closed door.

Panic drove him forward. Without thinking what he
was doing, he sprinted the last few steps and flung
himself at the door. It must have been on a pivot; to his
surprise, it spun him round and round, like the old-
fashioned revolving door of a hotel, before catapulting
him into the room beyond. It was fortunate for Michael
that the only occupant of the room (or, at least, the only
one worth talking about) was deeply involved in something else, for he stood reeling drunkenly for some
moments — before scuttering like a frightened rabbit to
the nearest hiding-place.

This was a large, richly carved cabinet of dark bog
oak. Michael propped himself in the shadows behind
it, catching his breath and trying to still the beating of
his heart, before daring to peep out again.

The room was splendidly furnished in a rich Gothic
style, like the inside of a castle, with many heavy
tapestries and screens; the high, vaulted ceiling was
decorated with birdlike masks. A high-backed chair on
a dais — again, richly carved with fierce, hook-billed
birds — suggested a throne.

But the piece of furniture which dominated the
room was an enormous desk set in the centre. It was lit
by flaring torches held in the hands of a pair of magpie-
men. They were standing so impassively that at first
Michael mistook them for statues — until he noticed
a nervous twitch rippling across one piebald cheek.
They were staring straight at the door, and he realised
that they must have seen him enter, but they were
apparently programmed only to act as lampstands:
they said no word.

The man seated at the desk had his back to Michael
and his head bent, so it was impossible to see his face.

All that was visible was a long, thin hand emerging from the sleeve of the black robe he wore. Strangely, although it held a swan's-quill pen — with which its owner was busily writing in a leather-bound volume — the hand was gloved.

Michael stared, fascinated, wondering where he had seen the glove before. Then it came to him: it belonged to the foreigner he'd seen earlier that day — the man with the chauffeur-driven black Mercedes.

He was just puzzling over this when there was a tentative tapping at the revolving door.

'Now I'm for it!' Michael said to himself, crouching into the deeper shadows behind the chest. Recalling the footsteps which had followed him, he waited tensely for the moment of betrayal.

'Come!' The remembered voice sent a chill down Michael's spine. Without looking up, the man at the desk dipped his pen into a silver inkwell and continued to write.

Slowly, the revolving door went into motion. Reaching an alarming speed, it plummeted the chauffeur, Tracey, into the room.

Michael hardly recognised him. The snooty self-importance of the man behind the wheel was gone. He was no longer in smart uniform; he still wore grey, but his garment was shapeless, almost as if he was clad in a piece of sacking. His highly polished boots and neat breeches had been replaced by a pair of sandals, which revealed feet that looked none too clean.

Stumbling almost to his knees, Tracey struggled to keep the balance of the tray he was carrying. Succeeding — just! — he gripped it with trembling hands, at the same time making an effort to stand to attention in his old way.

'Sir!' he gasped.

'*Sire!*' the man at the desk corrected him coldly. 'Here, I am a king. Have you forgotten where you are?'

Tracey made no reply. His shoulders drooped and his hands trembled more violently, causing the contents of the tray — row upon row of white-shelled eggs — to rattle together.

'These — these are ready for the — the incubation chambers, sire,' he ventured.

'Put them down.' A gloved hand gestured indifferently towards a space upon the desk. Tracey rid himself of his burden with relief. Stepping back, he raised his hand in a poor copy of the old chauffeur's salute.

Halfway to where the peaked cap should have been, the hand stopped. He glanced towards the cabinet. Michael swallowed hard.

But if the chauffeur knew he was there, he must have decided it was better to say nothing. He finished the salute and withdrew, leaving the door to spin behind him.

A heavy silence followed, broken only by the scratching of the quill pen. The magpie-men stood motionless. The light of their torches glimmered on the white eggs on the tray. Hidden behind the cabinet, Michael gazed at the eggs with curiosity.

Another sound intruded upon the quiet of the room: a feeble rustling noise, like the scraping of dead leaves left hanging on the branch in autumn, or the fearful scuttering of a mouse disturbed behind the wainscot. The sound was coming from above Michael's head.

Glancing up, he saw that he was not the only living being to be sheltered by the cabinet. Along its top, fidgeting nervously as they eyed the eggs, perched a long row of birds. From their size and shape, they could have been starlings; but if they were, they had lost the starling's jaunty posturing, the bright, iridescent sheen of its speckled feathers.

'Why don't they fly away?' wondered Michael, for it was plain from their uneasy movements that the birds were unhappy where they were. Beyond the magpie-men's heads, an arched window stood open to the sky; it would have been easy for the birds to make their escape.

Then one of them half-stretched its wings, and Michael saw that its flight-feathers had been cut. To make doubly sure it couldn't get away, its leg was tethered to the cabinet by a short length of fine chain. Its companions were held captive in the same way. One or two had lost all hope and dangled, lifeless, from their fetters.

The man at the desk took up an ebony ruler and drew a line. Then he laid down his pen. Immediately, a terrible stillness fell upon the birds.

The man's gloved hands reached out and pulled the tray towards him. He studied the rows of pale-shelled eggs.

'What shall we try this time?' he enquired of the silent tension in the room. 'What mix would make an interesting effect? What do I require? Will it be one of your kind?'

The magpie-men winced.

'I think not. Your type are rather too numerous.' A dry laugh issued from the Bird King's throat. 'Man-clone? Bird-clone?' he mused. 'Decorative or useful? Which will it be?'

A dark shadow flew up the wall and hovered menacingly as the Bird King pushed back his chair and rose to his feet. With a swish of his cloak, he moved to one of the ornate screens and set it aside, revealing a large showcase full of stuffed birds. What made these

birds different from those collected in a museum, Michael
noticed, was that each and every one was a grotesque
mongrel. Ducks had been crossed with sparrows,
pigeons with flamingos, an eagle with a wren — to the
benefit of neither.

There was nothing there, it seemed, to inspire the
Bird King. He replaced the screen and crossed to the
cabinet.

Consternation broke out amongst the ranks of
dishevelled starlings along the top. In vain they fluttered and struggled on their chains. A long, gloved
hand reached up. Michael cowered in the shadows, his
eyes squeezed tight, his hands over his ears to block
out the pathetic pleading of the birds ....

When at last he dared to look again, it was all over.
The tragic prisoners had settled back to apathy. One of
their number, the unlucky victim, was gone. Its chain
dangled uselessly. Something like a needle on a syringe,
with a scarlet tip, lay abandoned on the desk. The eggs,
newly injected, flushed pink with borrowed life.

Carelessly, the Bird King tossed the empty carcass of
the starling, like a piece of spoiled rag, into a waste-bin
at his feet. Ringing a small brass bell, he sat down once
more, dipped his pen in the inkwell, and began to
write.

Tracey answered the summons so promptly that
Michael might have supposed he had been waiting at
the door, if he hadn't been as breathless as if he had
been running.

'Oh, sir! Oh, sire!' he burst out, ignoring the gloved
hand raised to silence him. 'The Magpies ... the Hawkbreed .... There's been an accident!'

'*What*! Those fools! Can they do nothing right?' With
a swirl of black velvet, the Bird King was on his feet.
Thrusting the anxious Tracey aside, he swept through

the door. It spun so violently that the ex-chauffeur found it almost impossible to follow. Finally, after many false attempts, he vanished too.

Michael waited just long enough to count to five. Then he was out of his hiding-place and making for the desk. Under the impassive gaze of the magpie-men, he searched the top. He ignored the eggs and avoided the bloodstained instrument; it was no use to him.

Eventually he found what he was looking for, in a drawer: a delicate pair of scissors, like those used for paring nails (talons! thought Michael cynically), but strong and very sharp.

Back at the cabinet, he worked feverishly to cut the chains from the fluttering birds. To his dismay, once they were free they perched motionless, in disbelief.

Then they rose in a cloud to circle the room — once ... twice ... three times .... Freedom and joy worked wonders. Despite being hampered by their stunted wings, they flew faster and faster. With a rush like a mighty wind, they poured through the window, up and away to the sky above.

'Well done!' Michael danced with triumph.

'Hey! You!'

Tracey had returned. Finding someone weaker than himself, he was eager for vengeance. Michael didn't allow the ex-chauffeur to get his hands on him. Thrusting the magpie-men out of his way, he sprang through the window after the retreating birds.

Too late, he saw that the fortress was built upon a cliff.

As the starlings soared upward, Michael went tumbling head over heels — down, down, down ....

A Boy and his Dog
and a Druidess

*T*he dog shot out a long, wet tongue and licked Bridget's face.

'Get him off!' she spluttered, trying to rise. It was impossible; the dog was huge and he was sitting on her chest. She could tell by the vibrating of his body that he was wagging his tail. Nevertheless, she was anxious in case any false move on her part might cause him to use, instead of his long strap of a tongue, his very sharp white teeth.

'Here, Finbar! Leave it. Leave it, I say!'

The command was useless, so the owner tried another. 'Down, dog. Down!'

The result was immediate. 'Please get him off,' moaned Bridget, as the great hairy body flopped down on hers. 'He's crushing me to death!' By way of compensation, the tongue came out again and licked her chin. A cold, wet nose was pressed lovingly to her ear.

A hand came into view — a rather grubby hand, with clay under the fingernails. It closed around the piece of leather at the dog's throat, and with much puffing and heaving the animal was dragged away. Bridget sat up gratefully, wiping her face on her sleeve.

Unfortunately, Timkit chose that moment to descend

from his tree. Barking enthusiastically, the dog shot towards him.

'He'll kill him!' Bridget was on her feet.

'He's only a pup,' the dog's owner said apologetically. 'Finbar! *Finn!*' Putting his grimy fingers to his lips, he made the curlew's-cry whistle Bridget had heard earlier.

'I don't care what he is,' she snapped. 'He'll kill my cat.'

'More likely your cat will kill my dog,' chuckled the owner, as the 'pup' retired, whimpering, with a bleeding nose.

At last Bridget had a chance to study the boy more closely. 'Who are you?' she asked.

'Conn, son of Dair, son of Monghach Mór, Protector Elect of the Green Plains, Future Guardian of the Silver River, Heir to the Forest Lands, Prince of the Oak Grove,' said the boy, rather grandly.

It seemed a long title for someone so young; although he stood a good head and shoulders taller than her, Bridget guessed he was only about five years old. But his tunic, though torn and grass-stained, was richly embroidered, and he wore a wide gold band upon his tousled head, so she presumed he must be telling the truth.

'Men call me "the Acorn",' he added with a grin.

'I suppose everything is bigger here,' Bridget said to herself, her gaze shifting from the large child with his enormous wolfhound puppy — the size of a calf — to the taller-than-usual trees into which Timkit had returned for safety. She recalled tales Grandfather had told them of hidden lands and ancient times, when gods and heroes stood taller than normal men.

'Don't see much of my father,' the Acorn was saying ruefully. 'He's always away at war. Don't see much of my grandfather, either. He's too ....' He searched for the word. 'Too high up. Besides, as the Rules command, I'm fostered. They say it's safer.'

'Rules?' Bridget was beginning to feel sorry for this oversized small boy. He seemed lonely, somehow. Dog at his side, he was twirling a primitive leather sling loaded with a pebble. Aiming at a robin perched on a nearby furze, he fired — and missed. Bridget was reminded of Michael. Despite her disapproval of such weapons, she felt a rush of affection for the boy.

'Why safer?' she enquired. 'Aren't you just as safe at home?'

'Because my father's enemies don't know where to find me, of course,' Conn replied. 'But it's not fair,' he added plaintively. 'Most boys of my age get sent to a princely rath, where there are lots of other boys and they can have fun, hunting and wrestling and playing hurley. Thanks to the Rules I have to follow because I'm a prince, where do they send me? To a boring old Druidess — for *Education*. Which reminds me ....' He dived behind the furze bush and produced a leather bucket on a rope. 'I have to fetch her water from the lake. Her well-water is stagnant again — no use for Divination, she says — and she can't carry heavy buckets because of her rheumatism.'

'Does your father have many enemies?' Bridget enquired, when Conn — after the third attempt — had filled his bucket and they were both seated by the shores of the lake. The mist bridge had melted away as if it had never been, and the sun shone brightly overhead. Conn seemed in no hurry to return to his adopted home. He had produced a bronze hook on a piece of string and was attempting to catch a fish, without success. ('Not biting,' he explained. 'Wrong sort of worm.') Finbar was snuffling around in the bushes, but Timkit remained where he was, eyeing them all suspiciously from the branch of a tree.

'Of course.' Conn turned large eyes, blue as the sky, towards her. 'Anyone of any importance has enemies, and has to go to battle. It's part of the Rules. Besides, what else would there be to do? At the moment my father is busy with the evil Bird King of the Mountains. He's a powerful sorcerer, and he's a big challenge. My father will overcome him, of course,' he added hastily.

'Oh?' Bridget ran her fingers over the many flowers on the bank. She wondered if they were real flowers, or if they had arrived there by accidental magic, like the ones shaken from Frosty Meg's pipe on the far side of the lake.

She would have liked to ask more about the evil Bird King of the Mountains, but at that instant Finn put up a leveret and rushed off into the forest, barking. With whoops of joy, Conn abandoned his fishing and followed. He had forgotten the bucket. Sighing, Bridget picked it up and, with Timkit at her heels, followed more slowly.

Had it not been for the repeated curlew-cries and the hysterical yapping, she would have lost her new companions altogether, for the forest seemed trackless. All around, the tree-trunks rose high and smooth as columns, with a thick roof of gold-green foliage shutting out the light. Beneath, the carpet of undergrowth was particularly prickly. Timkit kept spitting and shaking his paws. Being barefoot, Bridget lost quite a lot of water from the bucket.

When at last silence fell, she was overcome by panic and started to shout Conn's name. To her annoyance, she was immediately answered by a triumphant curlew-call from just behind the bush where she was standing. Fighting her way round it, she found boy and dog,

breathless but happy, tussling over the limp body of
the hare.

'It was so young, you might have let it live.' Bridget
stared regretfully at what remained of the little beast.

'The pot must be filled,' Conn answered, rather
pompously. 'Finn and I are young, too,' he explained.
'Father says opponents should always be well-matched,
both in the chase and in battle. It's one of the Rules.'

Bridget felt like saying something rude about the
Rules. She suspected she wouldn't see eye to eye with
Conn's 'important' father. What had happened to his
mother, she wondered? She didn't seem to get a
mention.

There was no point in arguing. Already, Conn had
strung the leveret's legs together with his piece of
fishing-twine and tossed the body over his shoulder.
With Finbar still jumping and snapping at the prize, he
led the way. Timkit and Bridget, with the bucket,
trailed behind.

Now that there was someone who knew where he
was going, paths seemed to appear from nowhere,
sprouting from unexpected places and twisting and
curling between the trees. Conn moved with elaborate
caution; not a twig snapped, scarcely a leaf rustled,
beneath his sandalled feet. Occasionally he stopped to
aim at a bird with his sling, but usually the bird flew
off unharmed. If Finn tried to follow it, Conn called
him back with the curlew's cry.

'Why don't you whistle for him, like other dog-
owners?' Bridget wanted to know. By now she was
finding the call monotonous.

'Too obvious. It would draw the enemy's attention
to us. Anyway, it's our special call — Finn's and mine.
You can use it sometimes, too,' he added generously.

Bridget tried, but the sound she made was nothing

like a curlew, and Conn began to say 'Shh!' urgently, so she gave up. The feeling of urgency was catching. She found herself looking this way and that, imagining that there might really be hidden enemies amongst the trees. When Conn grabbed her arm and pulled her down behind a clump of brambles, she almost screamed aloud, fearing the Bird King himself was about to pounce.

At Conn's signal, they both raised their heads and peered across the brambles.

A broad shaft of sunlight was glancing through the treetops, highlighting a large clearing and scattering gold-dust on the trampled grass. In the sun-shaft, clouds of midges danced. The end of the clearing was marked by a row of ash saplings, planted so evenly and so close together that Bridget supposed they must have been put there for a fence (though what they were meant to keep out, or in, she couldn't tell). A makeshift hut with a sagging roof stood in the centre of the clearing; nearby, overhung by a twisted hawthorn, was a stone-rimmed well. There were a great many earthenware pots around the well; all of them were broken, suggesting that someone was in the habit of losing his or her temper and smashing the dishes.

The hut had no chimney, and no windows that Bridget could see. Its door was covered by a shabby leather curtain, painted in blue with magic signs or sigils. Above the door hung a wickerwork cage, occupied by a sulky-looking, moulting pigeon; against the door-frame leaned a birch broom, so encased in cobwebs that it looked as if it had been some time since it had been used. As there was no chimney, a fire had been built outside the hut. The wood was green, so it was belching smoke and looking as sulky as the pigeon.

The oddest woman Bridget could have imagined

was attempting to get it to burn.

She might have been fifty; she might have been a hundred. It was hard to tell, for her hair was dyed a vivid scarlet. There was so much of it that, in order to see, she had piled it high into a haystack of ringlets, knots, plaits, and tendrils, making her look top-heavy. To add to the effect, clusters of dead leaves, feathers, twigs, and dried flowers were stuck here and there amongst the curls. A pair of wishbone earrings dangled from her ears, and a long necklace of knucklebones clanked upon her breast.

Like the entrance to her dwelling, her face had been painted with sigils; but smudges of soot and dirt, and other signs of attempts at domesticity, had made the sigils rather blurred. Long soot-marks down the sides of her shapeless garment showed where she had wiped her hands. The garment was so tattered that you could see her bony limbs beneath. It looked as if she probably slept in it, never changing to a fresh one, not even on Sundays.

'My Guardian!' Conn hissed in Bridget's ear. With a blood-curdling whoop, he sprang to his feet and, accompanied by the yapping dog, stormed the clearing. The woman gave a thin shriek and dived behind the painted curtain.

'Of course I knew it was only you. I foresaw you,' she protested, once she had been coaxed, still trembling with fright and muttering protective spells, back into the open.

'I knew you were coming, too,' she announced to Bridget. 'I've been expecting you. Let me see, now.' She closed her eyes and swayed a little. 'Was it a love potion you were wanting? Or was it poison?'

It was neither, but Bridget didn't like to say so. One glance beyond the curtain at the contents of the hut (all of which looked pretty disgusting and could only be of use for weaving some especially nasty spells) told her that the old lady, strange as she might look, should be treated with respect. Magic was crackling all round her. It was a more powerful magic than Frosty Meg's, and it was somehow muddled, which made it seem more dangerous.

'And how is my cousin Meg?' the Druidess enquired. (Another thought-reader, Bridget assumed.)

'She was very well the last time I saw her,' Bridget replied politely, trying hard to remember exactly when that had been. She was not a bit surprised that the two ladies were related.

'Hmm. Just remind her, next time you see her, that she has a wind-charm of mine which she hasn't returned.'

Conn, in the meantime, had set about mending the fire, lying on his stomach and puffing at the embers till they flared. With some skill, he gutted and skinned the hare and plucked the feathers off a wood pigeon he had managed to bring down. Laying skin and feathers carefully to one side, he added the meat to a large cauldron which was bubbling on a tripod above the fire, and threw the innards to the dog. Finn devoured the meal as if it was the first he had seen in his young life, growling at Timkit, who approached, sniffed, turned up his nose, and went to settle by the fire. Presently, a delicious smell of stew filled the clearing, reminding Bridget that it had been a long time since she had eaten ....

'Divination first!' the Druidess said firmly. 'It always gives me indigestion after dinner.'

'Must we? Can't we give it a miss? I'm *starving*. Besides, what's the use? You never see a thing,' Conn protested.

'Young man,' the Druidess told him, 'your father

sent you here for Education, and Education you will have. Like it or not, the subject for today is Divination. Where's the bucket?'

The lesson took some time to set up. The Druidess kept remembering things that she would need, sending Conn running to the hut for a stuffed weasel, a lizard's claw, some beetle-dust — then recalling that beeswax worked better and demanding that instead. She had great difficulty in deciding whether to use the white owl's feather which was decorating her hairdo, or a tail-feather from the black cock. In the end she settled on a feather that had recently floated down from the moulting pigeon's cage.

Just when everything had been carefully arranged, the water from the bucket had been poured ceremoniously into the well, and they were about to begin, a frog jumped out and upset it all. They had to start again.

Finally, the right words had been said; they had joined hands and danced round the well-head 'three times three', on the Druidess's instructions. They approached, trembling, to peer into the depths.

'Like I said — nothing!' Conn was holding his nose against the smell of stagnation, which was powerful.

'Have a little patience,' snapped the Druidess.

'I know what's wrong,' she declared, after they had been staring cross-eyed down the well for a full five minutes, seeing nothing. 'You forgot the nine hazel-nuts, you *amadán*! They're in the basket beside the mummified rat. Fetch them. Quick!'

Grumbling, Conn was about to obey, when —

'Look!' breathed Bridget.

A picture was forming at the bottom of the well. A face.

Bridget backed away. She recognised the face immediately — the black hair and beard, the sickly, pock-marked skin ....

'Who are you? What do you want?' she heard Conn asking, like someone in a dream.

The Druidess went berserk. Jumping up and down, she tore at her hair.

'Not a decent sighting in weeks,' she cried. 'Not a single revelation! And when at last one comes, what do I get but *him*!'

Shoving the children out of the way, she sprang defensively between them and the well-head. 'You get out of here, you nasty bit of work, you!' she screamed. 'You're not wanted. You're trespassing. Go back to your leaky castle and your unpleasant games with birds. You put a finger on him' — she pointed at Conn — 'and I'll ....' Grabbing a broken pot, she began to fling earthenware at the well.

Somehow the children got her away and sat her down. By now the Druidess was stiff as a ramrod, and moaning. The sigils on her face had started to melt; they were mixing with the soot and dust to run down her neck in muddy rivulets. Her hair, gone wild, was writhing like a nest of scarlet serpents, scattering feathers and dead flowers everywhere.

'The Acorn! The Acorn!' she kept whimpering. 'Root and branch! He mustn't get the seed!'

'Water! Quick!' gasped Conn. 'She's going into a trance.'

But neither of them dared go near the well. The Druidess was drumming the ground with her fists, swaying to and fro, and crying out about salmon, cuckoos, nut trees, and Stones of Seeing.

'Water mint! It's the only thing to cool her down. That, and a bucket of cold water down her neck. The river is quite close by. Come on!'

It was an excuse to get away, and Bridget knew it — especially as Conn had neglected to collect the bucket.

But, like him, she was only too glad to escape from the clearing. With Finbar and Timkit competing to go first, they gave the well a wide berth and slipped out through the ash-sapling fence, leaving the Druidess to her ravings.

Once on the far side, Conn regained his old bravado, running along fallen tree-trunks, leaping bushes, zig-zagging merrily amongst the trees. Haunted by the face at the foot of the well, Bridget watched him nervously.

There had been something different about the man from the black limousine — the one they claimed was a sorcerer called the 'Bird King' — when she had seen him pictured in the water ....

She shuddered. He had removed his dark glasses.

Such eyes! Piercing and far-sighted, cruel and hungry as a hawk's — searching, searching ....

As she followed the overgrown small boy — bright-headed, the golden circlet gleaming in his hair — Bridget realised who those eyes were looking for.

Conn! Protector Elect of the Green Plains, Future Guardian of the Silver River, Heir to the Forest Lands, Prince of the Oak Grove ....

Glancing up, Bridget saw that the trees on this side of the mountain were fading, too.

Root and branch! He mustn't get the seed!

In some way she didn't understand, the boy and the trees went together.

The child whom men called 'the Acorn' was in danger.

The Sign-Maker

*A*lthough he was slightly winded, Michael — much to his surprise and relief — suffered no hurt from his fall. He landed on a bed of fir-needles so soft and deep that it was like landing on a pile of duvets. Lying on his back to recover, he saw the reason. All around him, the fir trees were quite dead. Not a single needle remained upon their branches.

Through a network of bare twigs, he could see the steep cliff and the stern ramparts of the fortress from which he had jumped. Black ooze seeped down its walls. Surely that was a head — that tiny round bead leaning out of a window, far, far up?

'Better not stay here,' Michael said to himself. In next to no time, Tracey would be giving the alarm. Struggling to his feet and picking up his catapult, he set off as quickly as he could through the dead forest.

The stillness was oppressive. Not a leaf stirred, for there were none; not a bird, nor a mouse, nor an insect, nor a blade of grass. Life, it seemed, had abandoned the forest altogether. No doubt it had been smothered by the same black slime that flowed down the castle walls — for there was evidence of it here, too, lying in clots along the branches and oozing in sluggish streams down the tree-trunks to land on the forest floor. Michael did his best to avoid it.

What had happened to the starlings, he wondered?

No doubt, with the free highways of the skies before them, they had soared over the dead treetops, leaving the cruel place of their imprisonment far behind. 'I wish I could fly,' he muttered. The long empty alley-ways between the firs seemed to stretch into eternity.

When at last a sound reached his ears, he hurried towards it, not caring whether he was stumbling into danger.

Tap-tap-*tap* ... tap-tap-*tap* .... Surely such a regular noise must be man-made! Michael stopped to listen. Tap-tap-*tap* ... tap-tap-*tap* .... Yes, it was the sound of a hammer striking stone. And someone was whistling. Such a cheerful tune could only come from the lips of someone friendly!

Bursting out of the trees, Michael was almost blown back in his tracks by the force of the wind. He had to wrap one arm around a tree-trunk and lean into the blast. Struggling to keep his feet, he studied the scene before him with some amazement.

He seemed to have arrived at a quarry. Great slabs of limestone lay piled against one another, with here and there a single stone standing upright like a sentinel. Michael was reminded of the Burren in County Clare, where their father had taken them one day on an outing. There had been a fierce wind there, too. 'But not coming from *below*!' Michael thought, puzzled. Great puffs and gusts of wind were rising over the rim of the hillside where he was standing, breaking in waves against his knees. They brought with them an enticing smell of flowers and herbs and meadow-grass.

Dwarfed by one of the standing stones, a small, squat man in a peaked cap, with a long beard wrapped several times around his neck like a muffler, was whistling merrily to himself as he applied hammer to chisel and chisel to stone. Every now and then the

vigour of his hammering made his beard unwind, and
he was forced to stop and wrap it round his throat
again.

'Hi!' said Michael. With some curiosity, he approached
the little man to see what he was carving.

Because of the wind, he had to repeat his greeting
several times before the stonemason took any notice.

'Good day to you,' he said at last, pausing to wipe
his glistening brow with the end of his beard and push
his peaked cap (which was several sizes too large, and
bobbed up and down with every stroke) out of the way.
'And a fine hot one it is, too,' he added pleasantly. He
tucked the loose end of his beard down the front of his
leather apron and returned to his work.

Michael thought the wind, wherever it was coming
from, was rather chilly; but for once he had the tact not
to argue.

'Where am I, exactly?' he enquired. A place where
the wind blew upwards somehow didn't seem to belong
to the world as he knew it. The quarry seemed even
stranger than the Bird King's castle.

He had to repeat his question more than once before
he got an answer.

'*Exactly*? Now that's a hard one. Very hard indeed.'
The odd little man lowered his tools and pushed back
his cap so that he could scratch his head. Unlike his
thickly bearded face, his head was as bald as a snooker
ball, and just as shiny. He had very large, sticking-out
ears (useful for keeping his cap on) and bushy eyebrows.

'*Exactly* is always a difficult one,' he said, peering
out at Michael from behind his eyebrows like a squirrel
peeping through the foliage of a tree. 'Perhaps you
should consult the signposts?' he suggested, after a
pause for thought.

'Signposts?' Michael looked around.

'Of course. Isn't that what they're there for?' The little man nodded so violently that his nose disappeared inside his cap and he had some difficulty getting it out again.

'They give you every possible direction,' he informed Michael proudly, once he had extricated himself. 'This one I'm after finishing now' — he tapped the stone in front of him with his chisel — 'it says "Here"; and that one' — he pointed with his hammer — 'says "There".'

Michael examined both stones carefully, but as far as he could see they looked exactly the same. Both stood upright, and they were the same height and shape; each had a straight line chiselled partway across, from left to right, just three feet (a comfortable height for the carver) from the ground. The two lines were identical.

'This one says "Over" — that says "Under" — "Up" — "Down" — "Before" — "Behind" — "Near" — "Far" ....' Beard coiling and uncoiling, cap bobbing, the little man was darting among his masterpieces with all the enthusiasm of the expert. 'Take a look at these!' he exclaimed, sliding to a halt. '"Somewhere" and "Nowhere"! Aren't they well done? They're by far my best.'

Following, Michael was at a loss for words. He couldn't see a scrap of difference between any of the stones. If they were signposts, there was no indication of where they were pointing; the tops just went up, the bottoms down. As for the marks on them, Michael supposed they must be some sort of Ogham; but, as they all looked the same, clearly the writer hadn't got beyond the Ogham equivalent of the letter 'A'.

'That's the lot, now.' The little man wiped his hands on his leather apron. Taking off his cap, he fanned his face with it. 'So far,' he added, tucking his beard — which had become very unruly — firmly back into his apron.

'Well, I don't see where it gets me.' Michael was beginning to feel cross.

'It doesn't get you anywhere.' The bright squirrel-eyes regarded him through the eyebrows. '*Anywhere*!' the little man cried delightedly. 'That's a good one. I must make a note of it.' He tied a knot in the end of his beard as a reminder and, picking up his hammer and chisel, immediately set to work.

Michael flopped down on one of the fallen stones to watch. Through the sound of tapping, it came to him that he might have asked the wrong question in the first place.

'Where ... should ... I ... go ... from ... *here*?' he tried despairingly, attempting to fit his words between the taps and whistles.

'From here?' For once, the question didn't need to be repeated. 'Why, that's simple. Compared to "exactly", it's a piece of cake!' The little man laid down his tools. Tipping his cap to the back of his head, he looked at Michael critically.

'You won't be wanting to go backwards,' he said, cocking his head to one side, 'not after where you came from. So surely all that's left is forwards?' He indicated the rim of the hill. 'Backwards! Forwards! Do I have those? I do not.' Michael was forgotten again; the little man tied two more knots in his beard, and returned to work.

'Thanks,' said Michael. He crept to the edge of the hill and peeped over. The wind fought with his hair and made his eyes smart, but its scent was alluring, coaxing him to go on. The drop looked very steep. However, just a short distance from his feet there was a long, narrow cleft, like a goat-path, leading downwards.

'Is that the way?' he asked.

The stonemason was too busy to answer, so Michael

eased himself over the edge of the hill and stepped
onto the path. 'Goodbye, now,' he called back.

No reply. Tap-tap-*tap* ... tap-tap-*tap* ....

The path was even steeper than it had looked, and
the grass was short and springy, so that Michael's feet
kept running away with him. In some places he found
it best to sit down and slide on his bottom. So he had
little chance to see where he was going. In any case,
swirling pink clouds hanging above the valley blocked
the view.

The rock on either side sheltered him from the wind,
but the sun beat down upon him mercilessly; he began
to feel that going downhill was a harder task than
climbing up. He was glad, therefore, when he came to
a wide ledge, in the shelter of a rowan tree, where he
could take a rest.

He stretched out on a bed of grass and herbs. The
wind curled under the branches of the tree and fanned
his face. Through a shifting pattern of green leaves and
scarlet berries, the sky was an intense blue. Below him,
the swirling clouds had begun to clear, and at last
Michael was able to see where he was going.

Far down, woods, meadows, and lakes — tiny but
exquisite — were spread out like a relief map for his
inspection. A river glittered like a piece of tinsel in the
sun; beside it, Michael could just make out three dots,
no bigger than money spiders, moving along the bank.

'Whoever or whatever they are, I'll join them when
I've had a rest,' he told himself sleepily. Leaning back
against the bole of the tree, he closed his eyes.

If Michael had listened more carefully to his grandfather's stories, he would have known that the rowan
is a magic tree, and that it is not sensible to fall asleep
underneath it. Unfortunately, for some time, he had
been caught up in his own interests and opinions, and

had left the 'fairy tales' to Bridget.

He awoke with a start, to find that the weather had changed. While he had slept, the wind had dropped. A dense, damp mist clung to the hillside, making it impossible to see more than a few feet.

Shivering violently, Michael scrambled to his feet. Berries were pattering down on him from the tree. The branches shook. Squinting upwards, he caught a broken glimpse of black-and-white shapes swinging and swaying in the boughs like apes.

He reached for his catapult and fitted a marble into place — but it was too late. With jabbers of triumph, the magpie-men dropped to the ground and surrounded him. Michael had no chance to fire a shot. A net was lowered, and he was trapped.

He was dragged, bumping along the ground, all the way back up the hill to the place where he had started. The signposts were still there, but the cheerful little man with his hammer and chisel had disappeared.

At the edge of the dead forest, the magpie-men became uncertain what to do. They wasted some time pulling the net — which, by now, was fastened round Michael like a shopping-bag — to and fro between them. Tempers became frayed. Quarrels broke out, leading to scratched faces and bitten arms and legs.

In the end, the magpie-men settled for climbing up the nearest tree and hanging the 'bag' containing Michael from one of the upper boughs. Still quarrelling, they headed off in the direction of the fortress from which they had come — leaving Michael behind.

The Poet

*T*he three microscopic dots that Michael had noticed beside the tinsel river were in fact Bridget, the Acorn, and a poet. Finbar and Timkit were there, too, curled up close to each other in the sun (they had made a temporary peace agreement, as the same patch of sunlight was to both their liking), but of course they had been much too small for Michael to see from the mountain.

The children had met the Poet by the river. 'Water,' he had told them, 'is a great source of Inspiration.' As he had been asleep when they found him, Bridget assumed that Inspiration must come to him in dreams.

He was a tall, lanky man with a domed forehead and a mournful expression. His deep-set eyes had the faraway look of someone who is 'not quite there'. He was wrapped in a cloak striped in the seven colours of the rainbow. It was fastened by an elaborate filigree brooch — 'A gift,' the Poet assured the children, 'from the King of Munster, in gratitude for the ode I composed for him.' ('Actually, he stole it,' Conn confided to Bridget in a whisper. 'And the ode was very long and boring — I was there.')

Conn, it appeared, knew the Poet well (the Poet was in the habit of turning up in the Druidess's clearing every evening for a meal). He greeted him with all the titles appropriate to a major poet, which were even

longer and more complicated than Conn's own. They
didn't include a nickname, so Bridget decided it was
easier just to call the poet 'Poet'. In any case, it didn't
really matter what she called him, for he completely
ignored the fact that she was there.

'What about the water mint we were meant to collect?'
she asked Conn pointedly. But he ignored her too.

The Poet listened to Conn's tale of the face in the
well with feigned indifference.

'Of course, your Guardian's powers are slipping,' he
said. 'She is not as she was in days of yore. She is
getting old. Divination cannot be accomplished in a
pool of muddy water. The Crystal Fountain, the Nine
Nuts of Wisdom and the Noble Salmon are what you
require.'

'A salmon?' Anything to do with fishing caught
Conn's imagination. He had left his hook and line
behind in his hurry to escape from the clearing, and
there were no salmon in the river. So he took to tickling
trout.

'No, no! That isn't how it's done.' The Poet was
expert in the art of fishing, as in all things. 'You must
stroke his left side, not his right — and with a hazel
wand, not a piece of willow!'

'I'll stroke him any way I like.' Wet but happy, Conn
was giving his complete attention to the creature
basking below the bank.

These were boys' games, Bridget considered. It only
needed Michael to be with them, and she would be
feeling really left out. Not that she would object to eating
the trout once they caught it. (Timkit, too, was showing
an interest. Finbar, being a meat-eater, was asleep.) She
bitterly regretted not having had a taste of the delicious-
smelling stew in the Druidess's pot. To keep hunger at
bay, she reached into her pocket for an apple.

The sudden movement brushed one of the silver leaves out of her sleeve. Caught by a breeze, it floated off to land upon the water.

'What was *that*?' The Poet became very excited. Much to the children's surprise, he gathered up the ends of his cloak and sprang into the middle of the river.

'It's only a leaf,' snarled Conn. 'Now look what you've done!' he cried, exasperated. 'You've disturbed the trout.' A long, freckled body caught the sunlight as it streaked away.

'*Only* a leaf!' The Poet emerged further downstream, dripping but triumphant, the delicate silver object caught between thumb and finger. Weighed down by water (or by Inspiration), he had some difficulty climbing up the bank, and the children had to pull him out. '*Only* a leaf!' he repeated. 'Do you not know where this leaf has come from?'

Bridget opened her mouth to explain that it had been up her sleeve, and that originally it had come from Grandfather's tree. Sensing that she was wasting her time, she shut it again.

'This leaf,' the Poet was intoning, 'this small silver lung from a vital, gleaming bough, comes to us with a message — a message from the Lost Forest! If there is even one leaf, the Forest is *not* lost!' Overcome by emotion and unaccustomed exertion, he sat down.

'Do you mean there's a whole forest of silver trees?' Bridget asked excitedly.

'Alas — mislaid!' The Poet forgot himself enough to speak to her directly.

'Who mislaid it?' Bridget was puzzled.

'My Guardian, of course; she's always losing things.' Conn was becoming impatient with this conversation. 'Look!' he cried with glee. 'Your cat has caught the trout!' Indeed, Timkit had intercepted the fish in the shallows. Being, in his opinion, the rightful owner, he was reluctant to give it up ....

'Yes. I lost the Forest,' the Druidess admitted dolefully. 'Take your thieving hands off that fish,' she snapped at the Poet. 'It isn't cooked yet.' By the time she had recovered from her trance (without the help of water mint), the stew had been ruined; so — after some argument as to whether or not the fish should be used for Divination — Trout Stuffed with Nine Hazelnuts was on the menu. Conn was turning the fish, strung on a green willow wand, upon a hastily constructed spit.

'I didn't mean to lose it,' the Druidess added. 'It was an accident.'

'An accident?' Bridget was at a loss to understand how anyone — even someone as vague and forgetful as the Druidess — could lose a whole forest.

Dead flowers and feathers bobbing in her hair, the Druidess nodded. 'I only meant to hide it,' she explained. 'With that so-called Bird King turning his interests from the feathered folk to shrivelling up the leaves, I thought it wise to conceal it for a while. So I conjured up a piece of mist. The trouble is ....' Her hand sought her hairdo, absent-mindedly patting it into place. 'I can't remember which patch of mist I put it in.'

'Mist is an insubstantial medium,' the Poet said critically. 'It requires an *expert*.' He reached for the trout, and had his fingers slapped.

'You should have marked the mist with a sprinkling of honeydew,' he advised, hastily withdrawing his hand and licking his fingertips.

'You try finding a sprinkling of honeydew in the Misty Marshes,' the Druidess snorted.

'The Misty Marshes? Sounds like an adventure!'
Conn's eyes shone at the prospect of monsters in the
swamp, or drowned warriors who arose at midnight ....

'It's an adventure, all right.' The Poet glowered at
the Druidess. 'If you don't mind getting wet.'

'But I thought — you said — water was a source
of ....' Bridget lapsed into silence.

'What's so special about a Silver Forest, anyway?'
Conn wanted to know.

'Do you remember nothing of your Tree Lore?' the
Druidess cried despairingly. 'Ash has other uses than
for making hurleys, you know. And not every willow
wand becomes a fishing-rod! I suppose you weren't
listening, as usual. I don't know why I bother to teach
you anything.' She leaned over to box Conn's ears. He
ducked.

All trees were 'life-sustainers', the Druidess explained
— the silver trees in particular. 'For they have been
touched by magic, and protect the rest. Were it not for
our forest of silver trees, by now this self-styled "King"
would have turned the lands on both sides of the
Mountain into desert. If there's one thing he dislikes,
it's natural life, so he doesn't want it sustained at all.
The mishmash he makes in his laboratory — that's all
right, for he can rule it. *Real* life, with all its wonderful
complexity and power, he hates. He's scared of it.'

'Well, if he's scared he should be easy to overcome.'
Conn brandished the fish upon its spit.

'Did you never notice that it's when people are
scared that they're most dangerous?' the Druidess
asked scathingly. 'Oh, why did I have to go and hide
that forest — just when, I'm thinking, we're going to
need it most? One tree would be enough. A handful of
leaves would help.' Her hair tied itself into knots and
tangles with frustration.

Bridget said nothing. She put her hand up her sleeve and spread the remaining six leaves upon the ground.

'Where did you get these?'

It was as if the trees encircling the clearing held their breath. The fish was forgotten. Another supper was on the point of being ruined.

Slowly, the Druidess reached out and gathered up the leaves, smoothing each one with her crooked fingers. Under her hands they lost their tarnished look and shone once more. Laying them in her lap, she looked at them for a long time. Then, closing her eyes, she began to croon:

'Oak is strong, the rowan bright,
Ash is straight and brings the shower,
The yew tree is as old as Time,
But the Silver Tree — she has the Power!'

'They come from — from Grandfather's tree,' Bridget said with awe. How did the Druidess know the song? she wondered. 'But — I'm afraid it's dying.' Her voice broke.

The Druidess hardly seemed to hear her. 'I told Meg at the time,' she said. 'She wouldn't listen, for she had fallen in love with that young whippersnapper. Always one for the fellas, was Cousin Meg! "Let him take something back with him," she pleaded. "A twig; a sprout!" "They don't transplant," I told her. "He should never have come through the Mountain, anyway. Now that he has, we're bound to keep him." She was always a determined lady, was Cousin Meg, even when young .... "You'll be doomed to walk their world," I warned her. She didn't care. It's a wonder the tree has lasted so long in foreign soil .... But that's what drew a certain hawk-eye in that direction, I'm thinking.'

'What are we going to do?' All this poetry and past history was of little interest to Conn.

'Do? Why, find the Silver Forest, of course.' There
was prophecy in the Druidess's words. She stood
straight and upright as the young trees guarding her
clearing. Her red hair blazed. Even Finbar and Timkit
sat up and took notice. The pigeon forgot it was sulking; it flew down from its cage (which had a faulty
catch) and landed on her shoulder.

'An adventure! Hurray! That's better than education
any day. I must fetch my father's sword.' Conn vanished
into the hut and returned with something so blunt and
rusty that Bridget was sure it would be no use at all in
their defence. She guessed — quite rightly — that it
was a cast-off.

'You can come too, if you like,' Conn told her
graciously. 'But if there's any fighting you'd better
hide.' He gave the curlew's cry, and Finn came
bounding forward; to him, 'adventure' and 'walk' were
spelt the same way.

'Are you going to let them off on their own? Don't
they need adult supervision?' As children, dog and cat
disappeared through the ash trees, the Druidess gave
the Poet a poke. 'I can't go. Not with my rheumatism,'
she reminded him.

'I was in the midst of Composition.' Drawing his
rainbow cloak around him with dignity, the Poet rose
to his feet. His eyes had been closed, but it was true he
had been muttering a few words now and then. Before
leaving, he looked hopefully towards the fish, but it
was gone — stolen by Timkit, who had abandoned it
behind a bush as overdone.

Left alone with the pigeon, the Druidess stood for a
while, lost in thought. Presently, aroused by something
pecking at her hair (it was only the pigeon, trying to
reclaim a feather that had once been its own), she
crossed to the well.

An eye glared up at her from the muddy depths.

'I knew you'd be spying on us,' the Druidess told it. Tucking the silver leaves behind one ear, she struck a pose — rather in the manner of the Poet — and intoned:

'Oak, ash, and beech, they may unite,
Thorn weave thickets to make men cower,
The forests spread throughout the land —
'Tis the Silver Tree that holds the Power!'

A shudder ran through the stagnant water at the bottom of the well. The Druidess raised a bony shoulder and cocked her head flirtatiously.

There was a gurgle of liquid disappearing down a plug-hole. The eye went blank.

Backtracking

*B*eing suspended in a net from the branch of a tree gave Michael plenty of time to examine his bruises. They were many and colourful. When it came to being piebald, he rivalled the magpie-men.

Having felt himself all over to make sure there were no bones broken, he set about trying to escape. It proved to be impossible. If they were good at nothing else, the magpie-men were good at tying knots.

'I wish I'd remembered to bring my knife with me,' Michael said gloomily to himself. Under the circumstances, a catapult and a supply of marbles weren't much use.

He hung there, swaying gently in the strange upward breeze. Hours passed. At least, Michael supposed they were hours; but, as his watch had stopped as soon as he set foot on that side of the Mountain, he had no way of telling.

At one point he heard a merry whistle, and, peering through the meshes of the net, he caught a glimpse of the Sign-maker's cap passing by below. 'Sign-man! *Sign-man!*' he shouted, as loudly as he could. Without even looking up, the Sign-maker gave a cheerful wave and continued on his way in search of a suitable piece of limestone.

'Well, at least I don't have to go hungry.' An aching void in his stomach reminded Michael that a few cornflakes pushed around a bowl are scarcely enough for breakfast, but that at least he still had his marmalade sandwich in his pocket.

If anything, it was stickier than ever. Michael plucked off the bedraggled silver leaves, placing them one by one, like stamps in an album, on the piece of net in front of him. Apart from the stickiness, the sandwich tasted delicious. He had just licked his fingers, and was about to take a second bite, when he realised he was not alone. A large, fat pigeon was perched upon the network of rope above his head, bowing and cooing and extending its neck-feathers ingratiatingly as it bent towards him.

'Shoo! Be off with you,' said Michael. 'I'm not feeding the pigeons. There'll be no crumbs left over.' He gave the net a shake to dislodge his unwelcome visitor, but it merely fluttered upwards, then settled back on its perch and continued to beg. Deciding to ignore it, Michael bit deep into his sandwich. A feather, like a small curled moon, came floating softly downwards and landed in the marmalade.

This was too much! Michael seized his catapult and took aim at the bird. The net spun sickeningly, and his shot went wide.

Having lived with the Druidess ever since it emerged from the egg, the pigeon was well able to cope with sudden bouts of temper. It raised its tail. Its aim, unlike Michael's, was perfect. An unpleasant chalky-white blob landed with a splat on Michael's shoulder.

The pigeon had dodged all the Druidess's attempts to replace it in its cage. It had decided to explore the world before settling back down to domesticity (there were eggs on its mind, but they were for the future). With the Druidess shaking her broomstick and shouting things like, 'Come down at once, you silly grubber, or I'll put the fowl pest on ya!' it had soared over the ash trees and out into the forest.

The pigeon was accustomed to an open-clearing life, and it soon found that, from above, one tree looks much like the next. In no time at all, it was lost. It discovered, too, that the world can be an unfriendly place. It was mobbed by rooks, jeered at by jays, and warned off by blackbirds; then it was caught up in a large crowd of starlings who seemed to be in a hurry to escape from somewhere. They would have driven the poor pigeon hopelessly off course, if it had had a course to follow. Weary, ruffled, and with its small bird-brain completely in a spin, it was eventually lifted by a sharp breeze and set down on a bleak mountainside where the trees not only were all alike, but had no leaves at all.

'It must be winter already,' the pigeon thought. 'I've been flying for a long time!' It was about to do what any sensible bird would — put its head under its wing — when it noticed what looked like a large cage hanging from one of the trees. A cage meant 'home' to the pigeon, so it flew thankfully towards it.

The occupant of the cage, however, was not another bird, but a young human. Like all young humans, it was selfish and unreasonable and inclined to throw things. The pigeon was on the point of taking off again when a row of silver objects stuck upon the bars of the cage attracted its attention.

'I've seen something like those before,' it said to itself, dimly recalling the bunch of silver leaves stuck in the scarlet network of the Druidess's hair. It fluttered down to take a closer look.

Left to enjoy the remains of his sandwich undisturbed, Michael didn't much mind what the pigeon did with the leaves. After all, they were no use to him. He munched; the pigeon pecked.

Marmalade that has been in someone's pocket for some time, has been plunged deep into a pool of icy water, and has been squashed by someone sitting down hard on it, can become very like glue. The pigeon was finding it difficult to get the leaves away from the net. As it pecked, the rope — which was really only hay and rushes spun together — began to unwind.

'Good nesting material,' thought the pigeon (again, with eggs on its mind). Pulling out the fibres one by one, it bunched them — together with the silver leaves — in its beak.

Freedom can come hard. Before Michael had quite realised what was going on, the net had unravelled around him like a piece of knitting, and for the second time that day he found himself rushing rapidly towards the ground. By the time he had disentangled himself from the muddle, the pigeon was well on its way back to the Druidess's clearing, with a plentiful supply of building-materials in its beak. Michael, aching from head to toe, found himself alone on the hillside once more.

He was tempted to go downwards, down to the beautiful valley he had seen stretched below. But the way was steep, the wind was blowing more sharply than before, and he wasn't sure he had enough strength left for the descent. Besides .... He turned to look at the fortress, rearing black and grim above the naked branches of the trees. What other poor creatures were held captive there?

Here, it seemed, lay unfinished business.

'Just what *is* he up to?' Michael asked himself.

Before retracing his steps, he stocked up on his supply of ammunition. It wasn't hard to do, for the Sign-maker had left limestone chippings scattered everywhere. Then, gripping his catapult firmly in his hand, Michael made his way back to the Bird King's castle.

From the outside, it looked deserted; but Michael guessed there would be watchmen posted on the towers, and hidden sentries ready with a challenge as soon as anyone approached the door. Squatting down behind a dead tree, he studied the building for some time before spotting a possible way in.

It could be just another blob of the nasty slime oozing slowly down the walls; or it could be an air-vent or a drain, disguised by an elaborate carving of a gargoyle's head. There were many of these, hideous and birdlike; most of them were set high on the walls, out of reach, but this one was set lower down, and there was a framework of dead ivy clinging to the wall beneath it.

'It *might* be possible,' Michael muttered. Sticking his catapult in his pocket, he stole out of his hiding-place. Reaching the ivy undetected, he tested it for strength and began to climb.

His climb was worthwhile. It *was* a shaft, and it was just wide enough for him to squeeze into. Fortunately, it was quite short, so he didn't have far to crawl. It opened into a long corridor very like the one he had found on the other side of the building.

Michael peered this way and that; there was no one about. Gently, he let himself down onto the floor.

The place was unbearably hot, almost stifling. The stone walls to either side pulsed and throbbed as if they might explode at any minute. The flagstones felt warm under the soles of his shoes.

If Michael wanted to find out what was happening, he had struck it lucky. Without knowing it, he had landed right at the heart of the Bird King's evil enterprise.

The passage, like the one he had gone down earlier,

was lined with doors — all firmly locked, though it was hard to see how it was done; there were no key-holes. Putting out a hand in search of a key or bolt, Michael received a sharp shock. Not having met black magic before, he came to the conclusion that the doors were electrified, like a cattle fence.

This only heightened his curiosity. When at last he came to a door which stood open, the greatest danger imaginable wouldn't have prevented him from having a peep inside. Braving an intense wave of heat, he slipped through.

As he crossed the threshold, he was almost lifted from his feet by a bolt of power. It took him some time to recover.

The room was like a microwave oven, it was so hot and sterile. It seemed to be half-laboratory, half-hatchery. At one end, a mountain of glass vessels filled with a reddish liquid gurgled and gasped; beyond them were tray upon tray of large, identical eggs, all set on spot-less, chrome-plated tables and lit from above and below by weird blue lights. Down the centre of the room, between the tables, ran a metal walkway, so highly polished that Michael was almost afraid to set foot on it.

As he went, he studied the eggs. He had always been a bit of a bird's-nester. He had never actually collected eggs, for his mother had pointed out that each one contained the potential for new life and, with the exception of the hens' eggs they used for food, should be left alone. So Michael had contented himself with climbing into trees and hedges and observing nests. In this way he had come to know quite a lot about their occupants, and he was able to tell one type of egg from another. He judged, from their shape and markings, that these came from some sort of hawk — although how a hawk could lay such large eggs, he couldn't imagine; they looked big enough to contain a newborn child!

At the end of the walkway he found another open door, leading to a second room filled with identical hawk's eggs. Here the blue light was even more intense. Caught in its beams, the eggs appeared to be breathing.

Michael froze. Just a few feet away, a magpie-man was moving up and down between the tables, spraying the eggs with a mist-like solution from a cylinder strapped to his back. Absorbed in his task, he hadn't noticed Michael.

Backing hastily away, Michael looked round the first room for somewhere to hide. Apart from under the tables, there was nowhere, and he wasn't going to risk exposure to the dangerous-looking blue light. All he could do was dive behind the open outer door, pulling it back so that he couldn't be seen. At the same time he slipped one of the limestone chippings beneath the hinge, so that there was no danger of his being locked in.

He was only just in time; already the magpie-man's heavy tread was sounding on the walkway. He had been right in guessing that they had very small brains and were only capable of doing what they were told, he said to himself as he watched the creature stamping, dead-faced and flat-footed, towards him. All the same, as it placed its piebald hand upon the door he shrank back, certain that its blank eyes must find him in his inadequate hiding-place.

But, apparently, whoever had control of the creature's mind wasn't expecting an intruder. Zombie-like, it moved out into the passage, pulling the door closed behind it. Michael heard the lock click, but, to his relief, he could see from its position in the frame that his plan had worked. The door wasn't properly closed. He lost no time in returning to the second room.

In the first room, all had been quiet, apart from the bubbling in the glass tubes. But here there were persistent underlying noises. Faint scrapings and tappings were coming from inside the eggs. A sudden sharp crack sent Michael scurrying along the walkway.

He turned back just in time to see a head emerge.

What a head! It was hideous. Was it really possible for anything so young and new to look so old and ugly? Mesmerised, Michael stared at the bald, wrinkled thing swaying on its scraggy neck. Top-heavy and as yet without proper control, it did not try to heave itself out of the broken shell. Catching sight of Michael, it swivelled its face in his direction and hissed at him.

Involuntarily, he jumped back, knocking against a tray behind him. To his horror, he heard a second crack. Swinging around, he found himself looking into a face even more hideously malicious than the first.

Caught between the two creatures, Michael noticed that they were oddly human. Their cruel eyes, pouched and hooded in folds of pinkish-blue skin, were those of very old men made spiteful and ill-natured by the years. Tufts of stubby feathers, jutting here and there from otherwise-bald heads, suggested the remains of hair. Their hooked bills could have been large noses ....

Faced with the facts, Michael's mind raced into overdrive.

First, there had been the magpie-men. 'Magpies are cunning divils,' the Logman had told him once. 'Steal anything, they would, and pick the lock to get it!' Such creatures, given human hands but with their limited minds well under control, would make useful servants for an unscrupulous so-called king.

And these .... Michael recalled the words he had overheard in the Bird King's study: 'Incubation chamber ...

the right mix ... clones ....' There had been Tracey's frenzied announcement, which had angered his master so much: 'The Hawkbreed .... There's been an accident.'

These, then, must be the Hawkbreed: half human and half bird of prey, cruel, sharp-billed, no doubt with sharp talons which had yet to emerge; filled with hatred, even in the egg; designed, not to be servants, but to form an army. Bred for war.

Michael whipped out his catapult. A sharp limestone chipping laid the first head low. Then the second; then a third, which had just emerged. Under his onslaught, the blue lights fizzed crazily. The room went black. In the darkness, he fumbled for the first table and gave a heave. He heard a great rushing and scraping of trays as they slipped away, the splosh of the eggs as they hit the floor.

Table after table! Tray after tray! He was unable to see the devastation he was causing; but, judging by the sounds and the sulphurous stench, it was great.

Michael made a quick decision. He would deal with the first room in the same way as he had dealt with the second; then he would dash back to the air vent, and escape!

He had just reached the door when a hand grabbed him. Thin, powerful fingers dug into his shoulder.

'Got ya!' hissed Tracey's voice, close to his ear. 'The Boss isn't going to be too pleased with *this*. You come along with me. There'll be questions asked, I'm thinking.'

Michael had just time to hide his catapult in his pocket before his arms were pinioned behind his back and he was led away.

The Summons

*T*he Druidess was exhausted. She had a headache. For hours she had been fixing her attention on the bottom of the well, using every ounce of her magical strength in an attempt to search out the enemy and find out what was happening in his murky mind. She had been spectacularly unsuccessful. Spilt magic was zigzagging out of control all over the clearing, creating a series of miniature electric storms. Throughout the tempest, the Bird King had kept his thoughts well hidden. His ambition might be obvious, but exactly how he planned to achieve it was still a mystery.

'It isn't just a matter of killing trees,' the Druidess muttered to herself, 'for that takes time. Time, I suspect, is something he doesn't have.' She was kneeling on the wet grass, and by now her rheumatism had got the better of her. She rose creakingly to her feet.

'At least I've cast my shadow between him and that worthless pupil of mine,' she consoled herself, 'so the Acorn will be out of his sight for the time being .... I could do with a drink,' she declared, straightening her back with a popping of vertebrae and making an effort to sort out her hair. 'Divination makes me thirsty. Something stronger than well-water, I'm thinking. Is there a drop of home-brew left, I wonder?'

Blowing out small lightnings like so many candles, she was about to cross the threshold of her hut when a rustling in the cage above caught her attention.

'So you're back!' The greeting was not particularly welcoming, but the pigeon — having endured several thunderstorms on the way, and being busy building a nest — took no notice.

'What do you have there?' Reaching up with her birch broom, the Druidess gave the half-built nest a poke. The broom came away with a tacky bundle of silver leaves sticking to its bristles.

'Where did you get these?' she demanded of the pigeon, who merely mended the breach in the wall and made no reply. 'Oh, well, never mind. I've other ways of finding out.'

The leaves were gummed together by a strange orange substance the Druidess didn't recognise. Suspiciously she tested it with her finger, sniffed, and gave it an experimental lick. 'Ugh!' she said, spitting into the grass in a rather unladylike manner.

Marching to the well, she gave the leaves a good wash. Once they were clean and dry, she laid them out on the grass in front of her. They were dog-eared, ragged, but familiar — and the Druidess could read them like a book.

'You didn't get these from *our* forest,' she commented to the pigeon (who was otherwise occupied). 'They come from far beyond. Just where have you been scavenging?'

She sorted the leaves by shape and size, and set them out in a straight line. Immediately a faint breeze blew, and they were rearranged into a pattern.

'Mmm!' Head to one side, the Druidess studied the pattern. She gathered up the leaves, shuffled them like a deck of cards, cut the pack, and laid them straight. Again, the breeze blew and they were shifted.

'I see!' the Druidess said knowingly. She stood for some time, glaring, first at the leaves, then in the direction of the Bird King's castle. Very deliberately, she picked up the leaves and posted them one by one into the well. Then she leaned over to watch for the result.

The boy she saw, standing straight and pale before the dark, humped figure of the sorcerer, looked so much like a smaller version of Conn that it made the Druidess cry out. 'His hair is redder, though,' she said, peering, 'and he has more freckles. Oddly dressed, too. He's related to the girl, I'm sure of that.'

The Bird King leaned his elbows on the desk. He placed his gloved hands together. The fingers twitched slightly, but that was the only sign that he was agitated.

'So!' he hissed, his voice barely louder than a whisper. 'You thought you were being clever. Let me tell you that your action merely caused a slight blip in the production line — a tiny chip on the rim of my great enterprise. Still, such a misdeed must not go unpunished .... Are they hungry in the Nursery, Tracey? Are they bored? Are my little chicks lacking entertainment? What do you think?'

Tracey, standing behind Michael, made no reply; he merely shuffled his feet and coughed a little.

'Take him away.' The Bird King, it seemed, was becoming weary. Perhaps he was feeling ill, for he drew his cloak about him and shivered. Perhaps he knew that eyes were watching him from another place.

Tracey clicked his heels. He grabbed Michael by one ear and dragged him, still numb and pale, into the corridor. Michael went without protest, down corridor after corridor, in a maze. The Bird King's mirthless laugh still sounded in his ears. His parting words lashed like a whip: 'I know about the catapult in your pocket. Don't think it will do you any good. Not against *them*!'

At last, an iron door groaned open. Tracey gave

Michael a shove, and he fell through. The door clanged shut.

Overwhelmed by the noise and the stench of musty feathers, Michael found himself kneeling on a rickety flight of steps leading down to a large, high-ceilinged room. The walls of the room were white, a white so dazzling it hurt his eyes. Light poured in through row upon row of high glass panes. He couldn't see the floor. It was covered, corner to corner and wall to wall, with seething, half-feathered forms. Eyes bright with blood-lust glared. Sharp, hooked bills clashed; here and there a beak dug deep, and a partly fledged body shuddered and went down .... Michael gripped his catapult. He knew that what the Bird King had said was true. It was hopeless ....

'Enough!' screamed the Druidess. Almost diving into the well, she retrieved the leaves. Muddy and besmirched with pond slime, she stood for some time, very shaken. Then, getting a grip on herself, she turned to face the pigeon — and the problem.

'So it's war,' she mused. 'I am a pacifist,' she told the bird, who blinked at her in disbelief. 'I have been all my life. But if he's prepared for war, then let him have it! You're a carrier pigeon. It's time you did some carrying. You must take a message.'

The pigeon, however, was in no mood to act as pigeon post. Crouched low in its nest, it was concentrating very hard.

Standing on tiptoe, the Druidess parted the untidy mass of twigs and fibres and looked inside. Two pale, whitish ovals nestled beneath the pigeon's down.

'What a time to choose!' she exploded. 'Just when I thought you were going to come in useful.' Grumbling, she placed the silver leaves around the eggs to keep them safe and stomped into the hut. Presently there

were loud bangs and bumps, and the clatter of objects
hitting the walls, as she sorted out what she needed to
take upon her journey. She emerged, strung about with
items that to most people would have seemed utterly
useless, and stood for some time contemplating the
broom.

In the end she changed her mind. 'Too risky. Too
dangerous at my time of life,' she decided. 'Rheumatism
or no, I'll just have to walk.' She strode to the row of
ash saplings and gave one a tug. 'This, he is *not* having
as a hurley,' she declared, shaking out the roots and
trimming off twigs and leaves to make a staff.

'Happy motherhood!' she called sarcastically over
her shoulder to the pigeon. Taking up her clanking
burden and gripping her staff, she marched off into
the wood.

Birds shouted a warning at her approach. Small
furry creatures, alarmed by the noise, scurried off into
the undergrowth. The Druidess ignored them. She
moved purposefully through the trees until she came
to another clearing, in which stood an ancient oak.
Letting her burden drop with a clang, she took her ash
staff in both hands and knocked hard upon the hollow
trunk. A squirrel fled, chattering. A mouse peeped out
from a hole between the roots, saw who it was, turned
tail, and dived beneath the ground; there was an angry
rustling from the bats that roosted in the hollow.

'He can't be away from home,' the Druidess said to
herself. 'He never is.' She knocked again.

The birds ceased their twittering. The breeze was
still. Stretching up, the Druidess tore away a clump of
ivy from the crumbling bark and pressed her ear to a
hole in the wood. Loud snores, amplified by the oak,
blasted her eardrums.

'He's there, all right!' she declared, shaking her head

to rid it of the echoes. Placing her lips to the tube-like hole, she took a deep breath and blew.

At once, the snores broke into a series of snorts and snuffles. They were followed by a volley of coughing that shook the leaves.

'Who's there?' demanded a peevish voice from somewhere high up in the tree.

'Wake up, old man!' yelled the Druidess, battering the tree with her staff. 'You're needed.'

'Oh, it's you, is it?' The man at the top of the tree didn't sound too pleased. He coughed again, raspingly; the Druidess could hear him thumping his chest with a feeble fist. 'Go away,' he choked. 'I'm not receiving any visitors.'

'You'll receive me.' The Druidess was firm. 'I want to talk to you.' When there was no reply, she stuffed the end of her ash staff into the hole and rattled it about, causing an explosion of bats and other creatures living in the tree.

A commotion came from the topmost branches; the twigs heaved. 'They'll get in my hair,' Monghach Mór (for this was Conn's high-up grandfather) shrieked as the bats descended on him. 'They're in my beard!'

A sandal dropped through the foliage, followed by a cracked horn beaker and an iron pot half-filled with a congealed mess that might have been last month's breakfast. Jumping nimbly aside to avoid it, the Druidess noticed that a bronze clasp, highly decorated and rather pretty, had landed at her feet. Furtively, she picked it up and placed it in her hair.

Finally, a head — haloed with white hair and with a long white beard — made its appearance, framed in leaves. 'Just what do you want?' it demanded tetchily. 'If it's about my grandson, it's not my business, and I don't want to know. Talk to his father.'

'And why should I want to speak of him? Young scallywag! He's making no progress,' the Druidess informed Conn's grandfather. 'He's idle. He's forever mitching. No, you can forget that particular twig off your Royal Tree. It's war I've come to speak of.'

There was a very long pause, during which the head withdrew. 'Too old,' the ancient king was muttering. 'Lost the taste for it .... It's my son you want,' he called down to the Druidess. 'War is *his* business. He's always in the thick of battle.'

'He's away. He's got sidetracked. Off fighting the King of Lochlann, he is now, instead of attending to more urgent matters at home,' the Druidess said. 'He's gone beyond my reach. You have the Horn; you'll have to summon him.'

At this, Monghach Mór went into a painful fit of coughing. Wheezed remarks such as 'Short of breath ... out of practice ... Horn wants tuning ....' wove their way down through the leaves, along with some very uncomplimentary descriptions of the Druidess.

The old woman stood her ground. 'It's *your* job,' she persisted. 'You hold the Horn; you're the Summoner. You don't want the Bird King to take this rotten stump from under you, do you?' She gave the oak a thwack for emphasis. 'For if we don't act now, that's just what he's going to do. Come on, now. Blow that horn. We need a hosting — as many of the clans as you can reach. They can't all be fighting with one another, surely? Your son must have a few allies left?'

The commotion in the tree churned into a storm. Leaves fluttered, twigs snapped, boughs bent, as if two very large gorillas were wrestling in the topmost branches.

Monghach Mór's face, lips puckered, came into view, vanished into a backlash of branches, and reappeared again. A hand, gnarled and twisted as a limb of the tree itself, found its way through the foliage. With a monumental effort, it drew out a magnificent, gold-emblazoned horn.

'That's more like it!' Satisfied, the Druidess gathered together some of the leaves which had fallen in the turmoil and made herself a cushion on the ground. Plumping down, she began to sort out the bits and pieces she had brought with her. They included powerful amulets, herb dressings, corn-plasters, strong concoctions of tonic, home-made stink-bombs, and a large supply of something which looked highly in-digestible and which the Druidess referred to as 'Iron Rations'. All these, in her opinion, were essential for an army going to war.

At first, the notes from the Horn were muffled. 'Get your beard out of the mouthpiece,' the Druidess roared up at the old man. Then a shaky scale of notes, ending in something thin and discordant, arose — followed by a wheeze and a violent fit of coughing.

When at last the true blast came, rooks were blown upwards, clouds went off course, uprooted bushes rolled away, mighty trees that had stood for centuries shivered with anticipation. Caught in the impact, the Druidess turned three somersaults and came to earth in an untidy heap, stuck about with herb dressings and corn-plasters. 'Ouch!' she gasped, as a pack of Iron Rations obeying the law of gravity plummeted down and landed on her head.

All over the land, men stood as if in a trance. Then, with a great shout, every man reached for his sword. It was the Summons!

The Last of the
Natterjack Toads

"What sort of adventure do you call this?' Conn slashed savagely at a nearby bush with his father's sword. As the sword wasn't sharp enough to cut butter, the bush received little hurt beyond a few battered leaves.

'I don't call it any sort of adventure,' Bridget snapped. 'That was *your* name for it. You needn't have come if you didn't want to,' she added bitterly.

The pace was slow. Tempers were becoming frayed. One of the causes of this lack of speed was the wind, which was gusting round them, buffeting at their ears and pulling at their hair as if it wanted to drag them up into the clouds. 'Someone's left a wind-charm on the loose,' remarked Conn, who had some experience of such things.

The main thing slowing them down, however, was the Poet. Because they were walking by the river (in the forlorn hope that it would eventually lead to the Misty Marshes), he was insisting on stopping every few yards in order to compose another verse of an apparently endless ode. 'What's the ode about?' Bridget asked him conversationally, but he didn't consider it worth his while to tell her. 'My grandfather used to make up poems,' she offered; the information was treated with contempt.

'Can't we just leave him?' she suggested when, wrapping his rainbow cloak around him, the Poet settled on the bank for the fifteenth time.

Conn looked scandalised. 'You have to have a poet with you when you go on an adventure,' he said. 'You might need a bard to record your deeds. How else would anyone know you'd done them?'

Bridget bit her tongue rather than remind him that so far there had been no adventure. Nor did she remark that she thought it rather conceited of Conn to want a poem made about his deeds. She concentrated her attention on the scenery.

The river was growing narrower, which, Bridget supposed, must mean that they were coming to its source. They had left the forest far behind. The land-scape was desolate. One or two cracked alders were all that remained of the trees. Here and there a great rock jutted out of the windswept grasses, like an island fortress washed by waves. Even the animals were subdued. Finn clung to Conn's heels; Timkit, who was leading the way, stopped pouncing on crane-flies, which seemed to be the only creatures inhabiting the place, and walked more sedately. He was getting slimmer, Bridget noticed.

After about half an hour, the wind dropped and the river — which had shrunk to a mere trickle — vanished altogether, reappearing now and then in the form of scattered, rush-choked pools. With the loss of the river, the Poet's inspiration dried up as well. He became very moody and irritable, and inclined to kick the dog.

Despair set in. Under a leaden sky, the land around them was flattened to a pale, dried-up fen. 'It's as if everything — fresh water, colour, life — has been sucked out of it,' Bridget thought.

All of a sudden she found herself tripping over Timkit, who had come to a stop in front of her. Grabbing her blazer, Conn pulled her back. Finn sank down, whimpering. The Poet fell to his knees with a groan. Huddled together, they all stared at the place where land and sky were being rapidly swallowed up by a great, heaving mass of fog.

'The Misty Marshes!' Conn breathed. He drew his sword. Timkit jumped back nervously to avoid a long, damp tentacle which was reaching out to trap his paw.

'I — I think it's about time we turned for home,' the Poet quavered, struggling to his feet. 'My — my ode is at an end. After such a long piece of work, I feel a little empty; it must be well past dinner-time.'

This suggestion almost led to an argument, for — despite a general chattering of teeth, due to the waves of chilly dampness which had begun to creep around them — Conn was all for going on. Then, suddenly, they heard the faraway sound of a horn.

'What was that?' Bridget turned — only to find, to her amazement, that her companions were no longer there. Conn, Finn and the Poet were scurrying back the way they had come, as fast as they could.

'Hey!' she cried. 'The adventure — What about —'

'Can't stop. See to it later. Must answer the Summons. War!' Enthusiastically, Conn waved his sword; beside him, his wolfhound bayed loud and long.

'Wait for me,' gasped the Poet, struggling to catch up. Tripping over the ends of his cloak, he landed face-down in a pool of water. 'Stop!' he wailed, rising and giving himself a shake. 'The battle cannot begin without me. There must be someone to celebrate the victory in epic verse!' He abandoned all dignity and, lifting his cloak and tunic above his knees, raced after Conn.

'Well! It looks as if you and I are going to have to find the Silver Forest on our own,' Bridget remarked to Timkit, who was still faithfully at her side. Bending, she picked him up, for fear of losing him in the fog. Bracing herself for the ordeal, she took one step — then another. Soon she was lost from sight amongst the Misty Marshes.

If she had found it difficult to walk through the dark cave, this was much worse, and there was no firm hand on her back to guide her. The mist sucked at her face and clothing; it ran its clammy fingers through her hair and plastered the wet strands to her forehead. It sent small rivulets running down her neck, beneath the collar of her blazer, and sprinkled her eyelashes with water so that it dripped into her eyes.

Blindly, she stumbled forward. 'Trust the cat,' Frosty Meg had said, but Bridget dared not put him down; it was impossible to see her feet, let alone an animal in front of them. 'If only I'd brought a torch!' she said aloud, blinking and shaking her head to free her eyes from moisture. 'It would have helped a little.'

No sooner had she spoken than a beam of light appeared, just a short distance to her right.

'Aah!' Gladly, Bridget ran to it; but as she reached the spot, the light went out. A second beam lit up to her left; this, too, lasted only for a few moments, disappearing as soon as she got to it. A third, straight ahead of her, lasted longer. Then it too faded, leaving Bridget sinking up to her knees in a cold, wet bog. Somehow she struggled free.

A peal of laughter greeted her distress. Then came the voices.

'What a shame!' someone murmured sympathetically in her ear. 'Too bad,' agreed another. 'You should watch where you put your feet,' advised a third. Screams of mirth greeted the joke. 'This way,' encouraged the next voice, once the laughter had died down. 'Keep to firm ground.'

A light flickered briefly, but by now Bridget knew better. Taking a tight hold of Timkit, who clearly wanted to chase after the deceivers, she turned on her heel and walked deliberately in what she hoped was the opposite direction.

Immediately, there was an explosion of lights. They sparked; they fizzed; they showered down to jig around her. Fighting her way through a bombardment of hot embers, she managed to break free — only to find herself sinking into another bog. With cries of glee, the bright enemies streamed after her.

'Go away! Get lost!' she screamed, lashing out with her free hand. Caught in the crook of her arm, Timkit snarled and spat and showed his claws.

The cat had an effect. The lights vanished. The mist closed round Bridget. Limply, she picked herself out of the bog. She stood, sucking her fingers where they had been burnt by the attack, and waited for the fiery barrage to begin again. When it didn't, she began to creep forward, feeling her way to firmer ground.

Despite his much-improved figure, Timkit was growing heavy. Bridget was about to take a risk and put him down when she heard a new voice — quite different from the others — coming, not from the air, but from somewhere in the region of her toes.

'Do look where you're going,' it grumbled. It had a grating quality, like a file on sandpaper. 'I may not be too beautiful, but I can do without having my head caved in, if you don't mind!'

Hastily stepping back, Bridget made out two round yellow eyes regarding her severely from about four inches above the ground.

'Did no one ever tell you it was rude to stare?' the owner of the eyes asked coldly.

Of course they had, but Bridget couldn't help herself. At first, all she could see was the eyes, apparently suspended in the mist. Kneeling down and peering more closely, she saw that below the eyes were a wide, lipless mouth and a pair of narrow nostrils, set in a broad, flat face which seemed to be suffering from a bad attack of warts. Beyond the face was a humped back, also covered in warts.

'Are you a frog?' she asked doubtfully.

'A *frog*!' The creature seemed mortally offended. He swelled to twice his size, looming unpleasantly — if more visibly — closer. He had been right when he said he wasn't beautiful. 'I am a toad,' he announced huffily. 'A Natterjack Toad, to be precise. I am, as a matter of fact' — he swelled until Bridget was fearful he was going to burst — 'the Last of the Natterjack Toads.'

'Oh!' was all Bridget could find to say to this. Weakly, she sank to a sitting position on the soggy ground. As the toad could speak, she was wondering if he was under an enchantment. Recalling the story of the Frog Prince, she hoped fervently that she wasn't expected to kiss him.

For the time being, however, the Natterjack seemed to have forgotten her. He sat very still, eyes bulging, gazing straight ahead. Presently he rose onto his toes, like an ungainly ballerina, and tripped a few short steps forward. Opening his mouth like a cavern, he snapped up a worm.

'Well?' he asked, when — after a struggle — the flicking tail-tip had disappeared. He swallowed and gave a belch. 'What do you wish?'

'Wish?' The toad eating his dinner wasn't a pretty sight, so Bridget had averted her eyes. 'Wish?' she repeated, looking back at him.

The Natterjack sighed as if to suggest that the care of all amphibians lay on his warty shoulders. 'All toads have the power to grant a wish,' he told her wearily. 'Even Natterjacks. Even' — he sighed again — 'the Last.'

'Ah!' The answer was easy; Bridget didn't even have to think. She hugged Timkit's warm body to her and said clearly, 'I wish to find the Silver Forest.'

'Is that all?' The Natterjack showed no surprise. Perhaps, having lived so long (each wart represented ten years), he wasn't surprised by anything. 'I was wondering when somebody would notice it was missing,' he remarked dryly. 'Have you a particular need for it?'

Bridget had. But she didn't dare tell the toad; she felt that, as a resident of the Land Beyond, he might not approve. While they had been walking by the river, she had formed a plan. If she should find the Silver Forest, she would take a sapling — just as Grandfather had all those years before — and plant it in the yard to replace the old tree which was dying.

All she said to the Natterjack was, 'The Druidess wants it.'

'I thought she would, sooner or later! She shouldn't have hidden it in the first place.'

'Do you know where it is?'

'I ought to, considering she left me to guard it. I suppose she's forgotten that as well — and here I am getting goose-pimples in the fog!' (Was there room for goose-pimples between the warts? wondered Bridget.) 'Silly old fool!'

The Natterjack was silent for so long, contemplating the Druidess's folly, that Bridget thought he had forgotten her request. She was just about to remind him when he went up on his toes and caught another worm; with the end still dangling from his mouth, he muttered, 'Come along,' and walked away.

If she couldn't see a cat under these conditions, Bridget wondered, how could she follow anything as small as a toad? However, when the Natterjack turned round, she saw that he had a long yellow line down his back which shone out like a road sign. She had no difficulty at all in following him.

'What about —' she began anxiously, for as soon as they started, the mocking voices and flickering lights began again.

'The Pishoguers?' Coming from the Natterjack's wide mouth, the name sounded like an insult. 'Don't be minding them; they're nothing but a pack of silly spoofers.'

He led the way — very slowly. At the toad's pace, and with his frequent need to pause and catch worms, they hardly seemed to move at all. Timkit, in particular, grew very impatient; he complained loudly and bitterly.

'Please put that animal down,' begged the Natterjack, through a mouthful of worm. 'The way he's carrying on, I'm liable to become a cat's dinner, and I can't risk that. After all, I *am* the Last,' he said with dignity.

Bridget wondered what it must feel like to be the last of one's kind. Very lonely, she imagined. Against her better judgement, she unpicked Timkit's claws from her blazer and placed him on the ground. As soon as his paws touched the wet grass, he bounded away. And vanished.

'Now see what's happened!' Bridget turned angrily to the toad.

Her words melted. All of a sudden, the air was full of the tinkling of tiny bells. If she strained her ears, she could hear the words:

'The Silver Tree — she has the Power!'

'We appear to have arrived,' remarked the toad. Swallowing the worm, he gave a belch.

Bridget ran forward. Ahead of her, the mist was a-shimmer and alive with sound — faint, it must be admitted; but, if Grandfather's tree had sung like wind-chimes, this was the stirring of a mighty orchestra preparing to play the full symphony. Vaguely, through a white veil, she thought she could see the slender stems and graceful branches of silver trees. They waved; they beckoned; they enticed her to run deep into the wood, stretch out her fingertips to touch the leaves, dance round in circles to the music ....

'Wait!' The Natterjack's voice stopped her in her tracks. 'Magic is magic. Good or bad, black or white — or silver — it must be treated with respect. Listen carefully, now, to what I have to tell you.'

Reluctantly, Bridget sat down beside the toad. It was hard to concentrate, with the air so alive with silvery sound. But she managed to gather that, in order to lift the mist and make the Silver Forest shine out again, she must first walk right round the edge, 'following the path of the sun,' then go straight down the centre, 'without twist or turn,' and back again to the exact place where she had begun. It sounded quite simple, allowing for the poetic language in the Natterjack's instructions. Eagerly, she jumped to her feet, ready to begin the task.

The Natterjack called her back. 'Beware Shape-shifters!' he warned.

'Shape-shifters?' Bridget hesitated. Somehow, Shape-shifters sounded more sinister than Pishoguers. 'What are they?' She looked at the Natterjack, waiting for an explanation, but none came. The yellow eyes regarded her steadily from the mist.

Once more she started to move away. Once more, he stopped her.

'You'd better take the Stone,' he said huskily. 'If you're up against *him*, I'm thinking you'll need it.'

'Stone? What stone?' Bridget looked about. The mist swirled thickly. There were no stones on the soggy ground.

'The Toadstone.' There was a strange note in the Natterjack's grating voice; his eyes looked sad. 'Feel beneath my chin, and you will find it.'

Bridget knelt down. She didn't want to touch the toad's rough, carbuncled skin. But his eyes were pleading. Slowly she put out her hand and ran her fingers across the spot below his wide, lipless mouth. All the time, she was aware of his eyes watching her.

Amongst the many bumps and pimples on the coarse, dry skin, she felt one larger and harder than the rest. She mistook it for yet another wart; but, as she rubbed it, it fell into her hand, and she saw it was a round, green stone, about the size and shape of a sea-washed pebble.

Hearing a strange noise, she looked back at the Natterjack — and saw, to her horror, that he was melting away. Like a knob of butter dropped onto the hotplate of a stove, his feet and legs and warty back were spreading out and vanishing to leave no trace.

His eyes were the last to go. They remained for a while, gazing soulfully up at her through the mist .... Then they melted, too.

The Last of the Natterjack Toads was gone.

Shape-Shifters

*B*ridget gazed sadly at the spot where the Natterjack toad had been. The Toadstone felt heavy in her hand — almost as heavy as her heart.

'I didn't mean to do it. You asked me to take the stone,' she whispered. There was no reply.

'You've made a mistake.' 'You're on the wrong path.' 'Better turn back,' advised mocking voices from the air.

'I will not. Mind your own business!' Bridget turned on the Pishoguers. Determinedly, she made a deep cross on the ground with her heel to mark her starting-place. Obeying the toad's instruction to 'follow the path of the sun', she set out to encircle the wood in a clockwise direction.

Along the edge of the forest, the mist hung fragile as a veil of lace. All was quiet. Either the Pishoguers had taken the hint, or they were sulking. The trees had ceased their song; they stood very still, as if waiting for their release. They were barely visible, a mere glimmer at Bridget's side. 'Black or white — or silver — magic must be treated with respect,' the toad had said.

Bridget began to feel very lonely. Ugly though the Natterjack had been, at least he had been somebody to talk to. She missed Timkit terribly, and she was worried about him. 'He'll be hiding somewhere, ready to pounce out on me, just like he does at home,' she told herself hopefully. He did not appear.

Instead, as if they sensed her need for company, a small family of deer — buck, doe, and tiny wide-eyed fawn — stepped delicately out of the forest to join her. Utterly fearless, they led the way, pausing now and then to nibble the mist-sprinkled grass, occasionally looking back at her with their melting, dark-velvet eyes. Particles of light cast by the silver leaves dappled their coats and made them look like creatures of a dream. In a dreamlike state, Bridget followed them.

The spell was shattered when the fawn broke ranks and approached on wobbly legs to sniff her fingers. Entranced, she offered her hand to him, feeling his warm breath on her skin — until, overwhelmed by his own daring, he gave a buck and a bounce and scampered back to hide behind his mother. Bridget laughed aloud.

At this, the trees to her right gave a shudder. There was a discordant cry, and the deer vanished into the forest as silently as they had come.

'I'm sorry. I didn't mean to frighten you. Please come back!' Bridget ran to the margin of the wood and peered beneath the branches. Nothing stirred — just the faint drip of moisture from the boughs .... She was just thinking about entering the wood — 'Only a short way,' she assured herself — in the hope that she would see them once again, when there came a loud, imperious miaow from the direction of the path.

'Timkit!' Joyfully, Bridget doubled back. The cat was nowhere to be seen, but she thought she heard another mew from further along the track. With renewed hope, she continued on her way.

The next creature to pop out of the wood was a weasel. Weasels didn't have the same appeal as deer; Bridget was usually frightened of them. Once, at home, a weasel had got in amongst the hens, and Bob had shouted at her to keep away. 'That fella has sharp teeth. He'll bite the hand off you,' he had warned her.

However, this weasel had a charm of its own. White as ermine, with its mask and tail-tip smudged black as though by greasepaint, it had the comic face of a clown and the skill and lightness of a dancer. Skipping out in front of Bridget, it pirouetted, nose to tail; sprang, undulating, upwards; pretended to catch a leaf; then landed neatly on its two back paws. Front paws held out as if it was pleading, it balanced, waiting for applause. Then, in a flash, it made its exit back into the forest. Its painted face appeared, briefly, behind a tree, and withdrew.

Bridget stood rooted to the spot, hoping for a repeat performance. When the actor failed to make his second entrance, she crept to the tree where she had seen him last and peeped around the trunk. The mist swirled, white-backed, but it wasn't the weasel.

Again, Bridget thought she heard Timkit's voice behind her. She spun round — and almost tripped over a white hare, lying in a shallow scrape in the path. Alarmed, it leapt into the air, kicked out with its strong back legs, and dashed away.

Bridget, light-headed by now, chased it — around a corner and along the second side of the wood.

A hare is not an easy animal to catch (unless you happen to be a greyhound), so Bridget was foolish to try; but for some reason she couldn't help herself. Slavishly, as if playing follow-the-leader, she copied every twist and turn the animal made.

She should have realised that he wasn't really trying to escape, he loped along so easily in front of her. She should have noticed that with every zigzag he was leading her closer and closer to the wood. But she noticed nothing, until — *wham!* — she came slap up against a tree-trunk.

Bridget sat down, seeing stars. She had always suspected that Grandfather's tree was made of very hard wood; now she was certain!

By the time her head had stopped spinning, the hare was nowhere to be seen. This time she had no regrets. 'Good riddance to him!' she snapped, rubbing her nose (she was quite sure it was broken). Scrambling to her feet, she limped back to her chosen path. 'Nothing is going to make me leave it again,' she vowed.

But, when she turned the second corner, she realised to her dismay that she had spoken too soon. Tiny spiders were abseiling out of the wood, spinning their silken threads to form a complicated wicker fence across her route.

Of course, a spider's web is fragile and easily broken; but Bridget hesitated. She had watched the weasel without fear — even found him attractive — but spiders were a different matter. She had always, as Michael put it, 'made a fuss about spiders,' and she couldn't bring herself to go on.

She tried moving to the left, where the mist was at its thickest and the spiders had not ventured, but a burst of giggles from the Pishoguers forced her to change her mind. She was just easing her way towards the trees, in the hope of somehow getting round the obstacle, when once again she heard Timkit's voice and thought she glimpsed the tip of his tail further along the path.

'Trust the cat!' Frosty Meg had insisted. Without further thought, Bridget burst through the mesh of cobwebs. Timkit wasn't there. Almost paralysed with fear that she would put her hand upon their maker, she stood picking strands of gossamer from her face and hair.

The third side of the wood seemed to go on for ever. Bridget grew wearier and wearier as she trudged along. There was neither sight nor sound of Timkit anywhere. 'I must have imagined it,' she thought. 'Perhaps he's lost forever, and I'll never see him again.'

Overcome by exhaustion, she started to cry. 'Cry-baby! Cry-baby!' her brother would have mocked. 'All the same, I wish Michael was here,' sobbed Bridget.

And then, to her utter amazement, there he was — only a few yards away, amongst the trees! She started to run towards him.

A snarling, spitting bundle of fur leapt from an overhead branch and toppled her over backwards. Together they rolled along the path, round a corner, and on to the fourth — and final — side of the wood. By the time Bridget had freed herself from the cat's claws and picked herself up, Michael was nowhere to be seen.

But Timkit was very much there, large as life — even larger, for he had swelled with fury — and glowering.

'Timkit!' Bridget began indignantly. A look in the cat's green eyes made her stop.

Deer, weasel, hare, spiders — even Michael — none of them had been real. They had been ....

'Shape-shifters!' breathed Bridget, remembering the toad's words. Shape-shifters, trying to lead her astray — trying to prevent her from performing her task!

It was a very meek Bridget who followed the cat back to the mark she had left on the ground.

From then on, the job was surprisingly easy. Together, they crossed the wood, going straight down the middle, 'without twist or turn,' from one end to the other; the trees seemed to bend aside to let them pass. When they turned to go back, they could see their tracks — a pair of human footprints and four cat-paws — quite plainly in the sparkling grass.

Even before they left the wood, Bridget began to

hear a stirring in the branches, a low hum. Just as the leaves on normal trees uncurl and spread out in the lengthening days of springtime, so the chiming voices of the silver trees rose, sending out waves of song.

Bridget and Timkit came out into the open in a blaze of light and a great crescendo of sound:
'The forests spread throughout the land —
'Tis the Silver Tree that holds the Power!'
They stood enthralled.

The bleak landscape where the mists had lain was utterly transformed. Where there had been nothing but dank grass and half-choked sedge, flowers were sprouting and little copses of trees were glowing with new leaves. The glint of running streams was everywhere, and birds were bursting out of the woods, carrying the news of their release from enchantment to the rest of the Land Beyond.

'I wonder where the Pishoguers are now,' Bridget chuckled to Timkit.

To her annoyance, she saw that he was no longer at her side. Apparently the feeling of celebration had gone to the cat's head. Timkit had gone skipping across the flowery grass, and, with a cat's need to be higher than everyone else, he had scaled a perpendicular outcrop of rock. He eyed Bridget from above as she approached. Just as she drew near, he turned and, with a whisk of his tail, leapt down the other side.

There was a crack in the rock. Bridget squeezed through it and found herself in a long, narrow valley, closed in on either side by steep, high crags. In a split of blue, far overhead, birds whirled. At the end of the valley, a waterfall gleamed and was lost.

'Timkit! Timkit!' she called timidly. 'Tim, Tim, Tim!'

There was no answering miaow — just her own voice echoing back to her from the rocky walls.

On the Battlefield

*F*rom a portable cage held high on the shoulders of two piebald giants, Michael had a good view of the battlefield — a great plain that spread below the rocky escarpment where he was being held — and of the opposing armies.

On one side of the plain, row upon row of identical magpie-men were already in place, armed with poisoned spears. They were tense and twitching, waiting for the command to charge. On the other side, the clans of the Land Beyond were still gathering. Their army was much smaller and less disciplined than the Bird King's, but far more colourful. Gold torcs and armbands glinted; the sun shone down on bright cloaks and tunics and wild, outlandish hairstyles. Each warrior bristled like a hedgehog with all kind of finely sharpened weapons. Every now and then a small skirmish broke out as one clansman, eager for battle, found an excuse to argue with another.

They were led — or held loosely together — by a splendid auburn-haired man with a gold band around his forehead. As his chariot dashed to and fro, drawn by two plunging black horses, his long blue cloak floated out behind him like the sea. Beside him was a much older man, also wearing a crown. He was wizened and frail, with a long, flowing white beard which kept winding itself around the chariot wheels, threatening to bring the vehicle to a stop. Michael wondered why the princely warrior tolerated such a decrepit companion; but, as the old man was clutching an immense golden horn, he supposed he must be the herald.

Amongst the Bird King's army, overtopping the rest, stood his crack troops: the deadly Hawkbreed — steel-footed, steel-beaked, steely-eyed and grim. But there weren't many of them; Michael congratulated himself on the part he and his catapult had played in undermining the wicked sorcerer's plans for war.

He was still feeling stunned by the sudden change in his fate. One minute, he had been balanced precariously on the rickety steps above the Hawkbreed's 'nursery', all ammunition gone, utterly defenceless, waiting to be torn apart by cruel bills. The next minute, everything had stopped as the whole of the grim, grey fortress, from the deepest dungeon to the highest battlement, had screamed with warning sirens. Tracey had snatched Michael, quite literally, from the jaws of death, and dragged him before the Bird King — pale and icy with fury as he paced uneasily in his darkened corridors.

'This is your fault, you interfering little spy!' he hissed, rounding on the bewildered Michael. 'Thanks to you, the battle must begin before I am quite ready. But do not think that you have triumphed. It is not possible. I am all-powerful; there can be no doubt about the outcome of the fight. You may witness my victory before I find a fitting end for you. You may watch while your friends and accomplices suffer and die.'

Michael hadn't the slightest idea what the Bird King meant. As far as he knew, he had no friends and accomplices in this strange land. Helpless, but still clutching his useless catapult, he allowed himself to be stuffed into a tiny cage and hoisted onto the backs of two immense magpie-men, looming like monsters in the gloom. The Bird King lifted his ivory-topped cane and brought it down with a sharp *thwack* on the bearers' shoulders, making them scream aloud. Tracey added a couple of sly kicks of his own. Lurching sickeningly, Michael was carried out to war.

So far, the battle had not begun, and the Bird King himself had failed to make an appearance. Again and again the blue-cloaked chieftain charged towards the fortress, shaking his great spear and crying out his challenge. The enemy remained hidden.

'He's far too much of a coward to come out and fight himself,' Michael thought cynically. 'He'll stay where he is and let others do his dirty work for him.' It seemed that King Dair of the Land Beyond was of the same opinion; after shaking his spear a final time, he returned to the head of his army.

Silence fell upon the assembled troops. An uneasy stillness, like that which comes before a storm, broken only here and there, where an impatient warhorse tossed its head and pawed the ground, or a great wolf-hound, grown bored, yawned hugely. The ancient king, whom Michael had mistaken for a herald, fell into a doze. His coronet tipped drunkenly over his right eye. His son nudged him sharply awake. Muttering and fumbling, old Monghach Mór felt for his horn and brought it sleepily to his lips. His moustache became tangled in the mouthpiece, and the sound that came out was harsh and broken.

The next note rang true, sending a shudder through the Bird King's piebald army. As its echoes died among the surrounding hills, all faces turned towards an outcrop of rock which rose like a stage above the battle-field. Michael's eyes, following those of the warriors, nearly popped out of his head.

Onto the stone platform stepped two of the strangest figures he had ever seen. The first was that of a man. He was very tall and imposing, but he appeared to be moving with some difficulty and discomfort, and even at a distance Michael could see that his clothes were torn and his straggly hair and once-colourful cloak were caked with mud. The second figure was no less untidy, but as it seemed quite comfortable with its disarray, Michael supposed that must be its natural state. After peering long and hard at it, he decided that it was a woman.

Hand to his heart, the tattered man struck a dramatic pose. He cleared his throat and began to recite in a deep, monotonous voice. His companion raised her ash staff high. A wind came up, carrying the man's voice in the wrong direction and playing havoc with the woman's already untidy hair. Unconcerned, she twirled her staff like a drum majorette and let out a wild whoop. She was answered by a great cry from the opposing armies. The horn blew once more. With a crash like two express trains colliding head-on, the warriors charged.

Heads rolled. Blood spurted. Every now and then a poisoned spear found its target and a clansman clutched his chest, turned blue, and shrivelled on the spot. It soon became clear to Michael that he was in a very dangerous position, for his bearers — despite their orders to stay where they were — took fright and, in blind panic, dashed to the very centre of the fighting.

The fragile cage creaked and groaned above the heads of the struggling men. Its bearers' feet slipped and slithered on the bloody ground. Michael was tossed to and fro in his tiny prison, and his bones might have been broken had not an immense, red-bearded warrior blocked their path, plunging his sword into the chest of one of the bearers.

The magpie-man gave a groan and dropped like a stone. His partner abandoned everything and fled, leaving Michael to crash, amidst splintering wood and bending bars, towards the sticky ground. In no time he was buried beneath a pile of slaughtered piebald bodies.

Above his head, the fighting moved on. The sounds of shouts and screams and clashing of weapons faded into the distance. Michael, trapped in the debris of his cage, was left alone. A raven, searching amongst the bodies of the fallen, poked its head through and regarded him with a speculative eye.

'Shoo!' Michael said feebly. It withdrew its head and flapped away.

'Do you want a hand?'

The offer sounded so casual that Michael desperately gasped, 'Yes!', terrified that his rescuer might pass him over. He couldn't see the owner of the voice. All he could tell was that the boy — it sounded like a boy — had a dog, for he heard a scrabbling of paws and some loud sniffing sounds, and presently a very hairy face was pressed between the bodies overhead. A long, pink tongue found its way between the bars of the cage, and a slobbery kiss landed on Michael's forehead.

The dog backed away and sneezed violently. After some encouragement from its master, it began to dig again. The bodies fell away. Seizing a bar of the cage between its strong white teeth, the animal gave a heave. The bar gave way. A pair of hands — rather less white than the teeth — appeared, and Michael was dragged, with a cracking of more broken spars, through the gap and into the open. He was weak-kneed and battered; he could barely stand.

He found himself being regarded by two pairs of eyes — one pair brown and expectant, the other blue and far more critical. The owner of the brown pair wagged its tail. 'You remind me of a girl I know,' the blue-eyed one remarked.

If anyone had said that to Michael in the school playground, he would have flattened his nose. But this boy, although he looked much younger than Michael, was a good deal bigger than him. So he kept his hands at his sides. In any case, he noticed with some envy that the boy was armed. An imposing — though rather rusty — sword was stuck in his belt, and in the time it had taken to make his remark he had seen off one of the scavenging ravens with a powerful slingshot. It made Michael's catapult look tame.

Conn, the Acorn, studied his find once more. Except for the colour of his hair, the boy did look amazingly like Bridget. The similarity made Conn feel awkward. He was feeling guilty about abandoning Bridget, right at the edge of the Misty Marshes, to go to war.

'Well, at least you're not black and white,' he observed aloud. 'I was beginning to get spots in front of my eyes. I don't suppose you're worth a ransom?' he added hopefully. Michael didn't answer. 'No, I didn't think so. You'd better come along with us, anyway. And no trying to escape — it's against the Rules.'

'Where are we going?' Michael asked eagerly. Now that he was getting over the shock of his imprisonment and his fall, he rather hoped that they would join the battle. He could see himself and this young warrior (who wore a sort of crown, Michael noticed) fighting side by side, doing brave deeds .... 'I might get my own back on that nasty Bird King,' he thought, 'and on Tracey! *Especially* Tracey,' he said grimly to himself.

Conn, however, was under orders to go elsewhere.

'Will you stop waving that sword about when you don't know how to use it? You're in the way,' his illustrious father had snarled. 'I'm having enough trouble with your grandfather. Leave the field!' Even taking a captive hadn't overcome Conn's humiliation and disappointment.

Gloomily, he led Michael to the top of the rock where the Druidess and the Poet were watching the battle. At least, he figured, they would have a good view of the action, and they could cheer for their side.

It looked, as far as Conn could see, as if the clans were winning. They had begun to fight amongst themselves, which was a sure sign that things were going well. The magpie-men, not bred for war, were being defeated; they had started to straggle towards the fortress in a broken, checkered line. Only where the Hawkbreed still stood their ground were little knots of fiercely fighting men. Conspicuous among them were the auburn hair and flapping blue cloak of King Dair, Conn's father.

When Conn and Michael reached the top of the rock, they found a private battle in full swing. The air was positively crackling with broken spells, snatches of bad verse, and angry words.

'Keep that wind down! It's out of control! It's ruining the flow of my verse!' the Poet was shouting, his much-treasured sonorous voice shrill.

'That's not my fault, you *amadán*,' the Druidess snapped back. 'It has nothing to do with me. Can't you see it's a wild wind — a rogue wind-spell from the west? Call yourself a poet! You should know about such things. Oh, just wait till I get my hands on Cousin Meg! It's the spell I lent her, I'll be bound!' She waved her ash staff, making the wind a good deal worse. 'This is *her* doing. What business does she have sending a gale to interfere with *our* battles? Not that anyone wants to hear your doggerel verse, anyway,' she added spitefully.

Such a remark could only lead to armed combat. The Poet had just drawn himself up to launch a satire which would raise blisters on the Druidess's face; the Druidess, in self-defence, had pointed her staff at him and begun to mutter the spell that would change him into a block of stone — when a blood-curdling shriek, carried by the wind, made them forget their differences and turn to gawp in the direction of the Bird King's fortress.

'Look!' gasped Michael. He was finding it difficult to keep on his feet in the gale. But, clinging to Conn for support, he managed to stay upright long enough to point towards the tower.

A huge black bird, humped and menacing, was perched on the topmost pinnacle, swaying evilly. Its eye raked the pathetic remnants of its master's army. Upon its back, the human figure in its long black cloak looked like little more than a deformity amongst its feathers.

With a second harsh cry the bird took off, its great wings slicing the sky above the battlefield. The magpie-men, already in retreat, scattered, falling like bowling pins. Whimpering, the Hawkbreed fell to their knees and covered their faces with their claws. Even the bravest of the clansmen raised their shields in protection as the shadow of the great bird swept the ground.

On it came. Goaded by the sorcerer's ivory-topped cane, it soared high over the rock where the Druidess, the Poet, and the boys were standing. Up and up it went, rising above the buffeting of the wind ....

With a shrill scream, it plunged. Michael heard a

gasp; turning, he found that his new friend was no longer at his side. Feet kicking helplessly, fists flailing the air, Conn the Acorn, Protector Elect of the Green Plains, Future Guardian of the Silver River, Heir to the Forest Lands, Prince of the Oak Grove, was lifted by cruel talons and carried up and away — until he, the loathsome bird, and its wicked master blended to become a black spot in the sky.

Down on the battlefield, Conn's grandfather tore his beard; his father shook his fist and groaned. On the rock, Michael was hard put to control the wolfhound, which was trying to leap after its young master. The Druidess was beside herself with rage.

'Out of the way, you chanting fool!' she screamed, shoving the Poet aside. 'Your verse is no good now; it's action that is called for. We must follow them, catch them before they land, or we'll all be lost. Once that evil so-and-so gets the chance, he'll use his deadly magic to eat at the boy's heart like a worm in rotten wood. The Acorn will be turned into a hollow stump before he has the time to grow .... And, thanks to his laziness and messing about, I never even gave him Lesson One in Protective Spells!' she moaned.

With plenty of room to use her ash staff, the Druidess began to make great sweeping gestures. At the same time she uttered words so powerful that Michael — in spite of his hand upon the wolfhound's collar to restrain him — tried to block his ears, and the Poet, who was not used to such language, fainted.

A strange thing was happening. The wind, which all the while had been buffeting above their heads, gathered and bunched. In a corkscrew wave that collected every loose leaf and blade of grass for miles (and a few beetles and small birds as well), it spun towards the Druidess's staff.

'Hold tight!' she yelled. Reaching out, she grabbed Michael by the arm.

To his utter astonishment, he, the Druidess, and the dog were lifted off their feet and sent floating, like a bunch of hydrogen balloons, above the fortress, above the hilltops, up into the clear blue air.

The Valley of Lost Voices

*B*ridget crept on tiptoe down the centre of the valley. The rocky walls rose steep and bare on either side; at the far end, the waterfall gleamed, and was lost, and gleamed again. Even without shoes, if she made a sound it was caught up by the rocks and sent echoing on and on, until at last it faded beyond earshot; if she carelessly kicked a stone, the noise that followed was like an avalanche. Strange, she thought, that there should be so many sounds in a place that at first had seemed silent and still, the air tense with waiting. It was as if it needed only a human foot for the energy within the stones to be released, and for the memories they held to come flooding back.

Voices murmured in the cracks. As Bridget walked, snatches of conversation reached her ears. But, look as she might, she could see no one there.

'The pikemen will gather at midnight,' said a man's voice. 'You'd best be ready.'

'Kinsale! They're dropping like flies,' someone groaned.

'Help! I'm burning — burning!' a woman shrilled. Her cries sent shivers up and down Bridget's spine. *Trust the cat!* — 'Why has Timkit brought me here?' she wondered. 'The place is haunted.' But still the cat led the way, and she was forced to follow.

'I'm hungry. Please spare a crust,' a child's voice

pleaded. Bridget had nothing but an apple. She left it by the crack in the rock from which the voice had come, hoping the speaker would be satisfied.

'The Lochlannachs are come. The Skellig is dark; the lights are all blown out ....' Monks' voices intoned a prayer.

A hunt in full cry swept past, hounds baying, horns sounding, hooves clattering on the stones. Bridget stopped, fearful she would be trampled to the ground. But no horse was to be seen; no hound came into view. Red coats, black boots, white breeches were invisible. Timkit returned, weaving his supple body around her legs, and urged her onwards.

Not all the voices were sad. A man's rich baritone arose, singing a jaunty ballad; a woman laughed. 'Best pig in the market,' a farmer boasted. 'Fish! Fresh fish for sale,' a street vendor called.

'The ball was quite wonderful,' a young girl's voice enthused. 'The lights! The fashionable gowns! Such style! The Lord Lieutenant was there. Harry asked me to dance three times, and took me down to supper. I do believe he will propose.' Was that the same voice she had heard a while back, Bridget asked herself — shrieking with pain and crying out that she was on fire?

'One, two, three, O'Leary,
Four, five, six, O'Leary,
Seven, eight, nine, O'Leary,
Ten, O'Leary,
Postman!'

Their old skipping song! The echoes mocked as Bridget sang it too. Susan, her best friend in junior school .... One term, in the playground, they had sung little else. Bridget could almost hear the skipping-rope hissing on the rocks.

'One, two, three, O'Leary ....'

'Susan! Susie, you're back!' Bridget called delightedly.

'Back! Back! Back!' the echoes warned. It would be pointless to search the valley for Susan; her family had moved to Birmingham three years before. Since then, she hadn't returned.

'What was that?' Bridget stood stock-still. Somewhere a dog was barking.

'That's Grip's bark — I'd know it anywhere. Grip! Here, boy!' Eagerly, she started forward.

Timkit had heard it, too. Grip might have been his sworn enemy in life, but all was forgiven. Ears flat, tail curved in a bow, he streaked ahead. Amidst resounding echoes, bare feet and cat's paws went pattering across the rocks.

The mad dash led them to the valley's end. They stood looking at the waterfall tumbling over the stones. Somewhere beside it, high up, the dog went on barking.

'Grip! Grip! Grip!' No echoes now; they were drowned by the sound of splashing water.

'We've got to get up there,' Bridget said. She found she was speaking to no one. A small, spray-drenched, ginger body was already on its way.

Bridget hesitated. The climb was steep, the rocks were wet and slippery. To try to climb up — for what? an invisible voice? — was surely madness. Yet something told her she must try. 'You're here to help,' Frosty Meg had said.

'Well, I have helped a bit,' Bridget said defensively; after all, she had been the one who had found the Silver Forest and released it from its spell. 'Oh, and I forgot to take a sapling!' she lamented.

Still, now was not the time to think of that. Surely there was something more pressing to be done — or why had Timkit brought her to this forgotten, haunted place?

Determinedly Bridget put her foot on the first rock, looked for a handhold, and began to pull herself up.

The climb took much longer than she had expected. She was thankful she was barefoot, for that made it easier to gain a foothold on the slippery stones. Nevertheless, there were times when footholds and handholds seemed in short supply, and she had to cling to almost-vertical precipices while she fumbled for a way. She dared not look down, for fear of making herself dizzy; she dared not crane her neck to look up, in case the effort upset her balance and sent her tumbling to the sharp rocks below. In any case, the spray soon blinded her. The most she could do was peer through a watery film at the rock in front of her and hope that what she saw as something shifting and featureless was in fact solid, and had all the necessary knobs and crevices for her to hold on to.

The noise of the waterfall was deafening; no voices from the past, no echoes from another time bothered her now. There was just a continuous roar of rushing water.

'I hope Timkit is all right,' she thought. Cats were famously sure-footed, and they did have nine lives; she could only hope that Timkit hadn't been careless and worked his way through eight of his lives already.

When she heard Grip bark again, she realised she had arrived. With relief, Bridget rolled onto a flat ledge of cool, wet grass. Breathless, with her head spinning and her arms and legs feeling as if someone had spent a lot of time and effort trying to pull them off, she lay there for a while, just glorying in the fact that, for the time being, she could feel safe and had no need to go on struggling.

The dog's barks died to a whimper, then faded away altogether. From quite close by, someone spoke.

'Good dog, good lad. Sit, now. Stay!'

The words were so familiar — they had been so much a part of Bridget's childhood — that for a moment she just lay back, basking in their sound and smiling. The voice, too, had been part of her everyday life, until —

Bridget sat bolt upright and looked around. She was not quite at the top of the waterfall, but she had reached a grassy ledge, sheltered from the worst of the spray and noise by a massive boulder. To have soft grass beneath her was unusual enough, after the barren rock of the valley far below. But, jutting from one side of the boulder, there was a small, scraggy hawthorn. The fact that it bore creamy blossom and red berries at the same time was also unusual, but Bridget was too excited and amazed to notice that.

The voice she had heard — Grandfather's voice, which had been silent for so long! — was coming from a crack in which the tree was rooted.

Close by the boulder, Timkit was seated on the grass, washing himself. When he had every hair in place and was quite finished, he put in his tongue and began to pay careful attention to the crack. As soon as Grandfather's voice fell silent, he began to purr. The sound of his purrs vibrated upon the rock, rolling across its smooth, spray-drenched surface like the wooden wheels of an old cart rolling over cobbled streets, long ago.

'Timkit!' Bridget dared to whisper, despite the cat's rapt attention. 'Timkit, that was Grandfather's voice. Did you hear it?'

The cat paid her no heed. He rose and stretched. Down on his belly, he started to creep — soft paw following soft paw — towards the crack in the rock. The hair on his striped body, his ears, his whiskers, were on the alert. His eyes were fixed ahead. His attention was unbreakable. He might have been stalking a

mouse, but Bridget — now on her hands and knees,
holding her breath — guessed differently.

Then came the spring, the pounce! The cat's front
paws, soft as velvet, vanished into a hole under the
hawthorn's root. His tail-tip quivered, his body twisted
on its side with the effort, as his paws — claws safely
sheathed — drew out the prize.

'Is that what a voice looks like?' Bridget spoke with
awe. It was so small, so fragile, that if Timkit truly had
caught a mouse there would not have been much
difference.

Bridget knew that if something so delicate was to be
kept safe on the journey home, it would have to be
wrapped in a parcel. Her handkerchief did not seem
enough. There was a clump of spray-spangled ferns
growing in the shade of the rock, so she plucked a few
fronds, weaving them into a sort of basket. Round the
voice, she added leaves from the hawthorn and some
moss, which was growing on the stone, for extra padding.

At last, rising to her feet and holding the precious
bundle in her hands, she spoke to the voice of the dog
that was still hidden beneath the boulder.

'Good dog,' she told him. 'You did your duty; your
master will be proud of you. You guarded his voice well.
Lie still now, Grip. Good boy. Sleep, Grip. Go to sleep.'

There were tears in her eyes as she turned away
and, Timkit moving at her side, went to the waterfall's
edge. But her back was straight, and her foot was firm.

Most likely, the descent would not be easy. It would
be far more difficult than the climb up. Especially now
that she had a parcel to carry that must not be
dropped.

The Tree's Revenge

*T*hey were gathering speed. Michael tightened his grip on Finbar's collar. With his other hand he clung to the Druidess's ragged garment. The material felt worn and fragile between his fingers, ready to rip at any minute. He sent up a silent prayer that, in the excitement of the moment, the Druidess would not release her hold upon his arm.

'There they are!' The oddly shaped dot that was the Bird King, his horrible steed, and their captive came into view, growing larger as they sped after them. The Druidess gave a war-whoop and flourished her staff. For a second she forgot to chant the words of power, and they were sent plummeting down towards the treetops before, regaining her presence of mind, she sent them up again.

They were gaining! The wind whipped in Michael's ears and batted at his eyelids; it made Finn's tail stream out like a flag and twisted the Druidess's hairdo into such contortions that a shower of bone-headed pins, beads, feathers, and other paraphernalia came loose and pattered down to the distant ground like hail.

Ahead of them, the Bird King's hideous mount seemed to be in difficulties. It wasn't just that Conn had managed to free his sword and was hacking away at the creature's legs — causing little damage, but at least distracting it; also, it was having to weave its way through a snowstorm of tiny birds, all of them twittering with joy as if they had found a new way of living. The Bird King slashed out at the joyous mob with his ivory-topped cane, to no avail.

'Listen!' cried Michael. He tugged at the Druidess's fraying gown, making them loop the loop.

Carried by the silvery chimes of myriads of leafy bells, the strains of a song were floating towards them through the wind. The words were somehow familiar.

'Oak is strong, the rowan bright,
Ash is straight and brings the shower,
The yew tree is as old as Time,
But the Silver Tree — she has the Power!'
'That's Bridget's song — the one she hears when the wind blows through Grandfather's tree in a certain way!' Michael was so excited about being able to hear the words himself that he was wriggling violently, sending the Druidess badly off course.

'If you do that again I'll be obliged to ditch you,' she snapped. With some difficulty she set them to rights again.

'Beech is fair, the birch has grace,
The cherry tree is sweet of flower,
The yew tree is as old as Time,
But the Silver Tree — she has the power!'
A thousand twittering voices had taken up the song. The Bird King screamed in anguish, but the singing was relentless:

'Holly is sharp, and willow soft,
The hawthorn decks a fairy's bower,
Old yew spreads at the churchyard gate,
But the Silver Tree — she has the power!

Oak, ash, and beech, they may unite,
Thorn weave thickets to make men cower,
The forests spread throughout the land —
'Tis the Silver Tree that holds the Power!'

Michael was singing too, singing at the top of his voice, triumphant in his knowledge of the music and the words. Puffing out his chest, he sang the last line twice. As he finished the refrain, a great silver light arose and flooded the sky.

'The Silver Forest!' the Druidess cried. 'The spell is broken. It shines again!'

There was no more need for her words of power. Magic music filled the air. They drifted gently downwards, through the sea of crystal droplets that almost hurt the eyes, and landed gently on sparkling grass.

Blinking, they looked about to see what had happened to the Bird King.

He had not fared so easily. His landing had been anything but soft. Melted like wax by the silver light, his makeshift steed, its flight-feathers shrivelled to little better than broken bedsprings, had crashed to the ground. With its rider pinned beneath, it lay sprawled across a rock — a twitching, shapeless mass of putty.

Conn, with great presence of mind, had done a flying leap moments before the impact. He was flat on his back in a bed of furze, scratched but otherwise unharmed, crowing with delight as he caught dancing silver particles on his father's sword. Finn pounded towards him and flattened him further as he covered his master's face with doggy kisses.

'Catch him!' The Bird King had disentangled himself from his useless mount. Hobbling slightly and with torn coat, but still vigorous enough to make a quick getaway, he was speeding towards a ragged split between some rocks.

'Head him off!' screamed the Druidess. 'If he escapes into the Valley of Lost Voices, we'll never find him, for the echoes will never tell.' ('Tell ... tell ... tell ....' her own voice mocked her.)

'Stop lounging about. Use that famous sling of yours,' she snapped at her pupil, as she passed him. Conn arose from his prickly bed, red-faced and spiky from topknot to toes. He fumbled about amongst the thorns — in vain. His sling was gone.

'Never mind. I have my catapult,' Michael cried. Then he remembered he was out of ammunition.

Already, the Bird King had reached the crack in the rock which led to the Valley. Finn sprang after him, but was sent whimpering back by a blow from the ivory-topped cane. In a few moments the Bird King would be lost from sight, a mere dark shadow amongst the valley's many crevices and crannies. Crouched among the ghosts of the past, he would have time to plot his revenge and gain strength for his return.

The Druidess increased her speed, but her feet were hobbled by the torn hem of her tattered gown (Michael had ripped it during the flight), and she was brought to a sharp stop. The Bird King's mocking laughter rang through the overhanging rock. With a wave of his gloved hand, he turned to make good his escape.

His way was barred. Two figures had stepped out of the shadows and were resolutely blocking the narrow passageway that lay between him and freedom.

Caught in the silvery beam of light which flowed directly from the Forest, the girl and the cat looked much bigger than they really were. Timkit arched his back and spat; Bridget stood very still. Her eyes were dreamy. She seemed absorbed. She was carrying something hidden in her cupped hands. The light slanting from the Silver Forest shone on her mousy hair, making it gleam like polished copper. For an instant Michael did not recognise her.

The Bird King backed away, hissing like a snake cornered by a mongoose. Wildly, he looked about. He

needed desperately to find somewhere to hide —
somewhere where he could regain the sense of his own
power.

To one side the silvery forest blazed, making him
yelp with pain. But to the other, only a short sprint
away, stood a group of trees which had not yet been
touched by the general recovery of the land. They
were old, bare, and broken, many of them fallen; no
doubt they were victims of the Bird King's own black
enchantment. Hastily, the tip of his cane tapping on the
rock, he sped towards them.

Conn had not been idle. Where there is rock, there
are always chips and broken stones lying about. He
had been busy gathering as many as he could hold.

'Come on!' he shouted to Michael. 'We'll finish off
the old crow yet!'

The boys ran after the Bird King, beginning to pelt
him hard and fast. Sharp as they were, the stones had
no effect. One, from Michael's catapult, hit the sorcerer
full on the side of the head. It should have knocked
him senseless, and left a bleeding wound. It did not so
much as make a bruise.

The Bird King had reached the trees. Once again, he
flung back his head and laughed. His laughter echoed
along the Valley of Lost Voices, on and on and on ....

'Your puny weapons cannot hurt me,' he sneered.
'Only a Stone freely given, but causing the giver's woe,
can lay me low!'

He began, slowly and deliberately, to peel off his
gloves.

'Watch out for his claws!' the Druidess cried. Helpless, she screamed with rage.

A strange and terrible transformation was taking
place.

As the first glove came away, dropping to the

ground like a piece of discarded fruit-peel, it revealed
— not a human hand, but the thin, twisted, snake-
skinned foot of a bird of prey, topped by cruel talons.
At the same time, as if the evil magic was rippling up
the Bird King's arm, one side of the sorcerer was
changing. His mouth and nose were melting into a
curved beak, carbuncled but sharp. One eye had grown
round and lidless. Dusty feathers replaced half his
cloak. When he opened his mouth to speak, his voice
hissed and croaked.

'The old crow,' Conn had called him. And that was
what he was becoming. As yet, one half of him remained
a man, as he struggled to remove the second glove
with his clumsy bird-foot. Never had any marauding
rook or magpie seemed to have such longing for
destruction; never had any carrion crow, up to its beak
in death, been more malicious.

Michael recognised the bird he had shot at in Grandfather's tree, and renewed his efforts. Bridget came out
of her daze. She opened her mouth, like the Druidess,
to scream. Then something clicked in her mind, and
she shut it again. She became quick and efficient.

'Hold this,' she said to the Druidess, passing her the
thing that was hidden in her hands. She delved into
her blazer pocket.

'Only a Stone freely given, but causing the giver's
woe, can lay me low,' the evil king had jeered. *If you're
up against him, you'd best take the Stone ....* Vividly, Bridget
recalled the woeful expression in the Natterjack's eyes
as he sank beneath the soggy turf for ever.

'Use this,' she cried to Michael. She threw him the
Toadstone.

Michael took aim and fired. Sent speeding from the
catapult, the Toadstone found its mark, right between
the sorcerer's eyes — one birdlike, the other human.

Uttering a croak, the Bird King reeled back against a blighted oak.

Once, no doubt, it had been the proud prince of a mighty forest; now it was no more than a pathetic, empty shell, half-eaten by beetles. Even as the children and the Druidess watched, the dead tree came creakingly to life. Its naked branches began to test the air; fumbling with its broken twigs, it found the sorcerer's hood. It grabbed him by the hair.

As the Bird King fell back, the long-dried tree-trunk gave a crack and its bark split open. In vain, the Bird King tried to save himself. The hollow was too deep. He was swallowed up. The last the watchers saw was a gloved hand, struggling frantically for a fingerhold .... The tree closed its wooden mouth. And the gloved hand was gone.

Home by Swan

*C*onn's father held a great feast to celebrate what, he informed everyone, was 'a famous victory', one that would be 'sung by the bards down the centuries'. There was plenty of food — smoke from the cooking-fires rose high above the plain — but, having just seen the Bird King's terrible end, Bridget found that she had very little appetite. Besides, the piece of beef they put in front of her, though charred to a cinder on the out-side, was almost raw within. She had no knife and fork; apparently she was meant to eat with her fingers.

She gave the meat a cautious prod, burnt her thumb, and looked over to where Michael was trying to out-boast Conn in retelling their adventures. He was talking so much that he hadn't touched his food either. Bridget longed to give him a kick under the table, as she would have at home, but he was well out of reach.

Those warriors who could be spared from clearing the battlefield and setting fire to the Bird's King's fortress, which now blazed like a beacon on its high escarpment, had set up long trestle tables in a rectangle, leaving a grassy space in the middle where jugglers, acrobats, and fire-eaters could perform. At the moment, Bridget was being put off her food even further by the antics of a sword-swallower who was just a few feet in front of her.

On a raised dais at the far end of the rectangle of

tables, King Dair and the other chieftains were swapping stories and bad jokes while gorging themselves on huge legs of venison and ribs of beef, throwing the bones to the dogs beneath the table. Beside the High King — who had removed his battle-stained cloak and was resplendent in gold torc, armbands, and crown — sat a very beautiful lady; Bridget guessed she was Conn's mother, for she had the same fair hair and deep blue eyes. Every so often, when the boasting got too much, she would place a gentle hand on the King's arm to remind him of his table manners. On her other side, Monghach Mór, Conn's grandfather, his crown tipped over his nose, dabbled his beard in the gravy and sucked his fingers, but the lady seemed more tolerant of his behaviour.

The fire-eaters and jugglers finished their performance. They gathered up the small brooches, rings, and other tokens which had been thrown to them as their reward, and departed. The space was swept and cleared. Servants brought in a harp and an elaborately carved chair, and the Poet stepped into the centre of the rectangle. In honour of the occasion he wore a new cloak, freshly dyed, and a circlet of bog myrtle and hazelnuts rested on his brow. It looked so like the kind of wreath that people hang on their doors at Christmas, and it made him look so ridiculous, that Bridget got the giggles.

'Uh!' groaned a voice in her ear. 'Now we're in for a good few hours of boredom!' Bridget turned to find that the Druidess had seated herself on the bench beside her.

The Druidess hadn't taken the trouble to change her clothes for the occasion. Her party dress consisted of her usual tattered robe and unsavoury bone jewellery. However, she had made some attempt to tidy her hair, and had added one or two extra pieces of decoration to it. To Bridget's astonishment, one of these new ornaments gave a wriggle.

'What are you wearing?' she hissed.

The Druidess put up a vague hand, fumbled amongst the mess of curls, and placed an unfledged baby bird upon the table. Immediately, a second head appeared in her topknot, beak gaping as if hoping for a worm. She took it out and placed it beside its brother.

'Hideous, aren't they?' she agreed, as she and Bridget studied the naked, flabby-skinned little creatures. 'Their mother will have nothing to do with them. I always knew that pigeon would make a hopeless parent. Insists she has her career as a messenger bird to pursue! "You're no good at that, either," I've told her. "You're fired. I'm making you redundant." She takes no notice. Gadding about everywhere, she is. *Someone* has to mind the babbies!' Sighing, the Druidess replaced the nestlings in her hair.

The story of the battle, as retold by the Poet, was nothing like what had really happened, but as no one was listening it didn't matter.

'I suppose I'd better try to eat; it's only polite,' Bridget thought.

As she reached out for the piece of meat, a hand — supple and strong as a birch twig, brown as an acorn — grasped hers and held it tight. 'It is not wise to taste *their* food,' warned a familiar voice.

'Frosty Meg!' Bridget whipped round. The steak dropped to the ground, where Finbar, ever watchful for such events, gobbled it up. 'How did you get here?'

'More like *why* did you get here?' grumbled the Druidess.

The travelling woman ignored her cousin's rude remark. Unburdened by her usual bulky bags and bundles, she stood straight and tall, finer and more noble than the richest chieftain present. Light from the cooking-fires played on her colourful clothing. Her face was half-hidden in the shadows, so Bridget couldn't tell whether the ugly side or the beautiful was turned towards her.

'Your task is complete. Time to go home,' she said, fixing Bridget with her most powerful gaze.

Their leave-taking was rushed. Once they had made up their minds that it was 'time', the two ill-matched cousins hurried Bridget and Michael along. Michael didn't want to go at all, for he felt that there were still many brave deeds to perform. 'Besides, I haven't eaten yet,' he protested.

'You're not allowed.' Bridget took matters in hand by throwing his supper to the dogs. To her surprise, she received help from a strange quarter. A funny little man, with a long beard and a cap too big for his head, stepped out from amongst the feasters and ordered Michael away with the firm word 'Back!' and a gesture like a signpost. Michael appeared to know the man; he obeyed.

There was a last-minute panic when Timkit couldn't be found, but at last he turned up, curled fast asleep on Conn's mother's knee. Soon they were away from the hot, noisy bustle of the feasting-ground, standing by the cool waters of the lake.

A breeze ruffled the swans' feathers as they dipped and bobbed, probing the blue depths with their bills. Conn, Finbar, the Druidess and, rather surprisingly, even the Poet had come to see them off. A pigeon flew out of the trees with a clap of wings and strutted along the shoreline, bowing and cooing. Her arrival caused quite a bit of excitement in the Druidess's hair.

'You must come to my place sometime,' Michael said to Conn. 'We'll have some great adventures.'

'By the time you come back here, I shall be a mighty king and chief of all the Lands,' Conn replied. His tone was boastful, but Bridget thought she detected tears in his blue eyes as he bent to restrain his boisterous dog.

'We'll come back soon,' she promised, fondling Finn's ears. She felt a little tearful herself.

The Poet struck a pose and began his farewell ode (as usual, no one listened). The Druidess raised her ash staff in a smart salute.

'But how are we to get across the lake? There's no bridge,' cried Bridget. She appealed to Frosty Meg, who was standing apart from the other well-wishers.

The travelling woman stretched out a brown hand and beckoned. The largest of the swans left the group and sailed majestically towards them. At Frosty Meg's bidding, the children and the cat climbed onto the swan's broad back and nestled down amongst his feathers.

'There isn't any room for you,' Bridget pointed out.

'I'm not coming.' The two sides of the travelling woman's face were inscrutable.

'Not going!' The Druidess was aghast. 'What about your doom to walk the world? You can't go messing about with something like that, you know.'

'Till I'd served my purpose, the spell foretold,' Frosty Meg reminded her cousin, 'and done him a good deed. Well, I have. He's back where he's meant to be, and in good hands. He'll be in even better hands when this girl gets home.' She touched Bridget lightly on the shoulder. 'Anyway' — she bent to loosen the laces of her old boots — 'I've grown footsore with all my wandering. I'm due a rest. Surely you'll not be-grudge me that?'

'Rest, is it?' The Druidess snorted. 'If you stay here, you'll be forever interfering with my magic — *and* flirting with the fellas,' she added spitefully. 'Ah, well ....' She cheered up a little. 'Now that you're back, maybe you'll return that wind-charm you borrowed.'

A glint of amusement ran over the beautiful side of Frosty Meg's face.

'I never borrowed it,' she said. 'Don't you remember, you refused to lend it? Then you dropped the thing; it's been buffeting about the place ever since. Just as well, I'm thinking. It stopped that evil monster in his great fortress doing too much damage down below; and how else could you have harnessed the wind when you needed it to see him off?'

Just before the children left, the Druidess waded out into the water, her tattered robe inflating and bobbing around her like a balloon.

'I almost forgot,' she said, pressing a small bundle into Bridget's hands. 'I kept it safe. You know what to do with it when you get home?'

'Of course,' said Bridget.

The swan stretched his long neck. He unfurled his wings. Like the wheels of an aeroplane preparing for take-off, his black feet ran along the surface of the water. Then, with a flick of his strong pinions, he was airborne.

'Goodbye!'

'Goodbye!'

The Poet's farewell ode droned up to them for a while and then was gone. The farewell party became no bigger than matchsticks on the shore. The bright landscape of the Land Beyond faded beneath Bridget and Michael like a dream. They topped the mountains and saw the familiar fields and roads and farms of their own land far below, tiny and perfect as new toys.

∽

The swan set them down gently on the road quite close to home. When they looked round, he was gone. They hadn't even seen him fly away.

'*Did* it all happen?' Michael asked doubtfully — though he had many a scratch and bruise, received at the hands of the magpie-men, to tell him it was true.

'Of course.' Bridget nursed the package in her hands. The remnant of grubby, tattered cloth which had been wrapped around the moss reminded her of someone. It even had smudges of well-slime and pigeon-droppings on it — as well as a sigil, whose meaning remained a mystery.

Eager to be home, Timkit streaked ahead, ears flat, tail flying. The children followed more slowly, looking about them.

'The leaves are growing again,' Bridget said in wonder. 'Look!' She pointed to a nearby hawthorn, where clusters of pale-green buds were uncurling as if it were only early spring.

'That awful smell has gone.' Michael sniffed the air with relief. 'And there's no smoke coming from the Factory chimney. Are they on strike, do you suppose?'

'Michael ....' Bridget spoke hesitantly. She moved over to the grass verge; now that she was back in the real world, her feet hurt, and she was missing her shoes. 'Michael, how long do you think we've been away?'

Michael shrugged. He had no chance to answer, anyway, for whom should they see but Aunt Mary, hurrying along with her head bent low. She looked so unlike her usual neat, prim self that they stared at her for a moment before remembering their manners and giving her a greeting. She merely glowered in answer, and passed them by.

'What's up with her?' Michael stopped to stare.

'Have you not heard?' It was Bob, digging out the

ditch as usual and making his usual good job of it. 'Now that the Factory is after closing, your uncle has lost his job. No more chance for Her Ladyship to preen and swank in front of others. See what happens when you go missing,' he added dryly. 'Where have you been at all? There's a terrible to-do up at the farm on your account.'

'The Factory? *Closed*?' The children exchanged glances.

There was no time for further questions — for there was Mother, standing at their gate. As they ran to her, they saw to their dismay that she was crying.

'Where were you at all?' she demanded. 'You've been gone a whole fortnight! The gardaí have been scouring the countryside; you've been on the news .... All very well for Frosty Meg to assure us you were safe and in good hands! I've been nearly frantic! Then, when they found your shoes, Bridget, and your school-bag' — she turned to Michael — 'I didn't know what to think ....'

Then, all at once, fears and sorrow were forgotten. There were hugs of joy all round, with Timkit weaving step-dances about their ankles.

And there was a wonderful surprise. For when Mother stepped back, they saw Grandfather, looking fit and well, seated in his favourite chair in the doorway.

'Grandfather! Grandfather!' They dashed to his side.

Shyly, Bridget placed the package she was carrying in his lap. He looked up at her and smiled, and she saw that his face was no longer twisted. It was as it had always been.

'This is for you, Grandfather,' she said quite simply, 'from the Land Beyond.'

Bending, she placed a kiss on the old man's forehead, where the skin was soft and wrinkled and as warm as the lining of a well-worn coat.

Where Trees Grow

*T*his could be the end of the story. But it isn't — not quite. For, as Frosty Meg and the Druidess would agree, stories do not come to an end; they just change a little, and go on round.

'What *was* in that package?' Michael asked Bridget. She just smiled, and kept her secret.

And he didn't bother to pester her; for, just a few days after their homecoming, Dad returned from the States, and the reason for his going there was made plain.

He brought with him an armful of gifts and a great bundle of legal documents. The envelope containing the documents was addressed to Grandfather; it had been left at an attorney's office by his brother John, just before he died. In it was a letter which proved that the land where the Factory was built, and all its surroundings, had belonged to the Foley family all along.

'Didn't I always tell you it was so?' The Logman, who always knew everything, was paying one of his frequent visits to his friend. 'Your brother never sold that land at all. Didn't he know he hadn't the right? But he needed the money to go to the States, so he put it out on a long lease to a rich stranger who turned up that time you were away. I suppose it was the stranger who rented it on to that nasty foreigner with the gloves.

'That's what happens if you go gallivanting after women,' he told Grandfather severely. 'You should have done as I advised you and stayed where you belonged. The trouble with you, old man, is that you never listen. Your head is always in the clouds — or beyond the mountains!' he added meaningfully.

'You're right.' Grandfather's eyes sparkled with mischief. 'But, sure, if you go "beyond the mountains", look at the adventures you have along the way.'

The Logman snorted.

'Just what are we going to do with all this extra land?' Grandfather asked the rest of the family, once the Logman had persuaded his jennet to stop eating their hay and had driven home.

He spoke slowly and carefully, but ever since Bridget had given him the package from the Land Beyond, his speech had been improving daily. 'It's no wonder it's a bit rusty,' she said to herself, 'after being crammed in a damp crevice for so long.'

'Well, the Factory can go,' Father said. 'Ever since that foreign owner vanished and the business went broke, it's been nothing but an eyesore. It's not great land for farming .... You decide.' He turned to Mother.

'We'll have to buy out Sean and Mary's share,' she said, 'or they'll be forever at us to build housing estates. They're angry enough as it is, for wasn't Sean doing very nicely with the Factory there? What would have been on that land in the old days, I wonder?'

Bridget looked at Michael, and Michael looked at Bridget. Somewhere at the back of their minds, the Druidess was prompting.

'An oak wood!' they chorused.

'That's fixed, then. Once the Factory has been demolished and its mess all cleared away, you can set to work and plant some trees. It may keep you at home and out of mischief,' Father grinned.

So, with the help of Bob and the Logman, they did.

One thing, however, made the children sad. Even as their little oak saplings took root and began to sprout their first soft bronze leaves, it became obvious that the Silver Tree was fading to its end.

'I'll have to ask Bob to take it down,' sighed Mother.

'The Druidess said it couldn't last forever in our world,' Bridget mourned. 'Oh, how I wish I'd remembered to bring a sapling back with me! But when Timkit led me into the Valley of Lost Voices, I forgot. And after that, everything happened so quickly; we were home before I knew it.'

'Well, Grandfather's voice was more important,' Michael said. (So he had guessed what was in the package, after all! realised Bridget. He was much more friendly now that he had been to the Land Beyond, she thought — quite his old self.)

Then Michael looked at the old man and winked. 'When you made my catapult, what wood did you use?' he asked.

Grandfather looked up from playing with the new pup the Logman had given him to fill Grip's place. 'Guess!' he said.

Michael said nothing. He went to the centre of the yard and dug a small hole in the spot where the Silver Tree had been. Carefully removing the string, he stuck his catapult in the ground ....

The new tree's growth was rapid. Even before the year was out, its silver branches had begun to sing a song. Leaning far out of their bedroom windows in the evening, Bridget and Michael would listen ....

Then, with a grin at each other, together they would sing the words:

'Oak is strong, the rowan bright,
Ash is straight and brings the shower,
The yew tree is as old as Time,
But the Silver Tree — she has the Power!

Beech is fair, the birch has grace,
The cherry tree is sweet of flower,
The yew tree is as old as Time,
But the Silver Tree — she has the Power!

Holly is sharp, and willow soft,
The hawthorn decks a fairy's bower,
Old yew spreads at the churchyard gate,
But the Silver Tree — she has the Power!

Oak, ash, and beech, they may unite,
Thorn weave thickets to make men cower,
The forests spread throughout the land —
'Tis the Silver Tree that holds the Power!'

And when they were all gathered round the fire on winter nights, and Grandfather — his voice fully restored — would sing his ballads and tell his stories, the story Bridget and Michael would ask for over and over again was the one about the handsome young farmer who met, and fell in love with, a mysterious lady of the Sídhe whose face was half-ugly and half-beautiful. He would tell of how they journeyed together beyond the mountain .... But when he came to describe the Land Beyond, the children would start to fidget in their chairs.

'No, Grandfather,' they would cry, 'you've got it all wrong! It wasn't like that at all. We know. We were there!'

BY THE SAME AUTHOR
DON'T MISS ....

The Silver Chalice

It all started as an ordinary, boring class trip to the local museum. But suddenly a hand snatches the famous Silver Chalice, and both the hand and the chalice vanish!

Paul is the only one who can see the hand's owner,
a lost monk from the ninth century.

Take ghosts, Vikings, Hell's Angels and a spotted pig;
add one bespectacled boy — Paul —
and you have a roller-coaster ride through time and mystery,
where nothing is quite as you expect it to be ....

ISBN 0-86327-540-0

WOLFHOUND PRESS
68 Mountjoy Square, Dublin 1

THE RED BELLY TRILOGY
BY MARGOT BOSONNET

'Top marks, ten out of ten.'
Books Ireland

UP THE RED BELLY

The Red Belly gang — Felicity, Jonathan, Mackey, Muggins, Joan,
Dara and Orla — are spending their summer holidays in the
woods and up their wonderful tree, the Red Belly.
Join them as they tangle with a ghost,
get sussed nicking gooseberries, stage a disastrous production of
Blood and Guts on Treasure Island — and much, much more!

ISBN 0-86327-530-3

RED BELLY, YELLOW BELLY

For the Red Belly gang, the trouble started when Harold set up
a rival gang and called their tree the Yellow Belly.
They had to sort that little pest out — but Harold takes his revenge
in some very unexpected ways ....

And that's not all! What's lying in wait at the haunted gate-house?
Will Mackey and Dara ever learn to get on?
And why, oh why, are Felicity's parents making the gang
spend their summer tidying up horrible Old Fitzy's garden?

ISBN 0-86327-640-7

BEYOND THE RED BELLY

The Red Belly gang's summer is heading for disaster.
Property developers have plans for Conker Woods.

The battle is on!

The gang are desperate to save the woods. Protests, sit-ins,
even an alliance with the Yellow Belly gang —
will it all be enough to save the Red Belly?

ISBN 0-86327-755-1

The Drumshee Timeline Series

by Cora Harrison

'As a way of bringing a way of life long past vividly alive
... this cannot be beaten.'
Books Ireland

Nuala and her Secret Wolf
Nuala, an Iron-Age girl, adopts an abandoned wolf-cub,
but she must hide him from her family.

The Secret of the Seven Crosses
Led by mysterious clues, young medieval monk Malachy
searches for the lost treasure of Kilfenora Abbey.

The Secret of Drumshee Castle
Grace's struggle to escape her foster-parents' evil plots
takes her from Drumshee to the court of Queen Elizabeth I.

The Secret of 1798
Can Caitriona and her friend Serge, a young French soldier,
solve an ancient puzzle before the British track Serge down?

The Famine Secret
It's 1847, and blight, fever and famine have driven Fiona
and her family into the workhouse. But she dreams of escape ....

Titanic — Voyage from Drumshee
As nursemaid to two rich children, Kitty sets out for America
on board the greatest ship ever built: the *Titanic*.

millennium@drumshee
Emma needs all her computer skills to unravel
a thrilling cyber-mystery — and make a new friend.

The Drumshee Rebels
When Michael Collins came to Drumshee, Bridget never realised
how much danger he was bringing to her family.